FURY GODMOTHER

FEDERAL BUREAU OF MAGIC COZY MYSTERY, BOOK 2

ANNABEL CHASE

RED PALM PRESS LLC

CHAPTER ONE

"WHAT DO YOU THINK?" My mother stood in the center of the barn, watching John Maclaren, the carpenter, as he took measurements and made notes.

John cast a glance over his shoulder at her. "Everything looks to be in great shape from where I'm standing," he replied.

"Why, thank you," my mother said, smoothing her hair.

I rolled my eyes. "He means the barn, Mom."

John tucked his phone back in his pocket. "Shouldn't be too hard to transform into a living space for this young lady."

"Oh no, the barn is for my daughter," my mother said. "I live in the main house." She paused. "All alone."

I gave her a sharp look. "All alone with about a hundred other people?"

My mother waved a dismissive hand. "That's all temporary. You'll be moving out here and Anton and his family will be moving into their house as soon as the remodeling is finished."

"What about Grandma and Aunt Thora?"

"Well, they're old," my mother said. She flashed a flirtatious smile at John. "Like I said, temporary."

John only looked to be in his mid-thirties. I couldn't imagine he'd be interested in my mother. Then again, I couldn't imagine any man being interested in my mother. It was a wonder she and my father managed to get married and produce two children. I still suspected she used her magic on him somehow. Not that my father was a prize. Being married to a vengeance demon can't be easy. One critical comment about leaving up the toilet seat and you might find yourself bald by morning.

"I'll have an estimate for you by the end of the week," John said.

"That's wonderful, thank you," my mother said. "How long do you think a job like this will take?"

John tugged his ear, thinking. "We've got good weather these days and I've got room in my schedule, so not too long." He patted her shoulder. "Don't worry, Mrs. Fury, I'd be out of your hair in no time."

My mother frowned. "In that case, maybe we should hold off until winter, Eden. It's nice having you in the house."

"I'm in the attic on a mattress," I replied. "I don't even have a bed."

"Beds are overrated," my mother said. "Wouldn't you agree, John?"

Sweet Hecate, this was embarrassing. To his credit, John seemed oblivious. Or maybe willfully oblivious.

"If I'm going to have construction equipment back here, you might want to consider dealing with that old well," John said. "It isn't safe."

"What old well?" my mother asked.

"I noticed it on my way to the barn," John said. "I can recommend a water well contractor."

"I'm happy to consider *all* your recommendations," my mother said. "Keep 'em coming."

Ugh.

"Great. I'll be in touch," John said, and left the barn.

My mother waved after him. "Please do."

I waited until the carpenter was out of earshot to reprimand my mother. "Do you have to flirt with every male within arm's reach? For all you know, he's married."

"No ring," my mother said.

"He's a carpenter," I pointed out. "He works with his hands."

My mother smiled dreamily. "Good Goddess, I hope so."

Double ugh. "I'm going to work."

"Why don't you stay and have breakfast with us first? Aunt Thora is making slow-cooked oatmeal."

"I'm not hungry." That was a lie, of course. I was always hungry, but I had my eye on a scone at The Daily Grind, the best coffee shop in Chipping Cheddar.

"Tell your father I'll let him know what his half will cost for the barn when I get the estimate," she said.

"You can't just text him a screenshot of the estimate?" My parents divorced when I was ten, but they still avoided each other for the most part, despite living five hundred yards away. As part of the divorce settlement, they'd agreed to divide the old Wentworth dairy farm in half and my father built a new house on his plot, where he now lived with his second wife.

My mother pulled a face. "If I must."

"I'm happy to contribute to the cost," I said. "I have some money saved." Not much considering the high cost of living in San Francisco, but now that I was back in Maryland, everything was much more manageable. The cost of living was one of the few perks of being back in my hometown. I'd had no intention of ever returning to Chipping Cheddar, but an incident at work triggered my magic and I nearly killed my partner as a result. When the FBI discovered that I was better suited to the clandestine Federal Bureau of Magic, they sent me packing to the one place I didn't want to go —home.

"Don't be silly, Eden," she said. "You're down on your luck. The last thing your father and I intend to do is kick you when you're down."

"I'm not down on my luck," I insisted. My mother refused to accept that I wasn't fired from my job with the FBI.

"You lost your job. No boyfriend. Living with your mother at twenty-six years old." She clucked her tongue. "If that isn't down on your luck, then I don't know what is."

"Thanks for the pep talk, Mom. Now if you'll excuse me, I need to get ready for work."

"Yes, I suppose you should. We wouldn't want to risk you getting fired again. "

I stifled a groan and headed back across the grounds to the farmhouse.

Chaos reigned in the kitchen as everyone seemed to be trying to prepare for the day at the same time. Verity, my sister-in-law, was attempting to feed one child while another child clung to her leg.

Olivia, my five-year-old niece, was the one attached to the leg. She looked up at me when I entered. "You look creepy."

I shot a quizzical glance at Verity. "I look creepy?"

The druid shrugged. "Consider it a compliment. She's a big fan of creepy."

Ryan smiled at me and milk poured out of his mouth. Even the toddler seemed determined to be part of the mayhem.

"Ryan," Verity scolded. She glanced around the kitchen helplessly. "Where is your father?"

My brother Anton appeared in the doorway as if summoned. "You rang, my love?" He wore a T-shirt that read *something wicked this way comes*.

"You're wearing that to work?" my mother queried, also zeroing in on his choice of clothing.

Anton grinned. "What? It's ironic. They don't know."

What 'they' don't know at the office is that my brother is a vengeance demon, like our dad. Unlike our dad, however, Anton chose to work a normal job in the human world in the creative department for a small advertising agency. He recently admitted to me that he took small jobs in Otherworld to pay for projects like the home remodel, but he wasn't as keen on exacting vengeance for clients as our dad. It seemed that Verity was having a positive influence on my brother, at least as far as I was concerned.

"I'm heading out," I yelled over the din. "Everybody have a great day."

I hurried out of the house before anyone could force-feed me Aunt Thora's oatmeal. I needed room for that scone.

I left Munster Close and drove to the downtown area that overlooked the Chesapeake Bay. Even as someone who didn't want to live here, I recognized the charms of my hometown. The colorful and well-kept buildings around Pimento Plaza. The town had been settled by English Puritans searching for a better life in America. Formerly the home of many dairy farms turned cheesemakers, the human residents had no idea that the town is also situated on top of a dormant portal to Otherworld, the supernatural realm where members of my family are originally from. Even though the portal in this town is dormant, the mystical energy generated by the portal draws supernaturals to this area. My job at the FBM involves apprehending any supernaturals wreaking havoc in my jurisdiction and returning them to Otherworld where they belong. Supernaturals have long been permitted to live among the humans, as long as they don't flaunt their powers or upset the natural order of human life. Thanks to their penchant for wickedness, my own family teetered on the edge of what was acceptable. I hoped for my sake they continued to toe the line. The last thing I wanted was to be responsible for exiling one of them to Otherworld.

I found an ideal parking spot right out front of the coffee shop—a lucky break. While the town didn't get truly hectic until summertime when tourists seemed to outnumber residents, you still needed good parking karma to avoid a long walk on a busy weekday morning.

I pushed open the door and the aroma of fresh-brewed coffee filled my nostrils. As far as I'm concerned, The Daily Grind is the only place for coffee in town. After experiencing three years of excellent coffee in San Francisco, I couldn't subject myself to the sludge that passed for coffee in most places here. I'd only been back a few weeks, but I'd spent enough time here that the staff already knew me.

"Good morning, Eden," a voice chirped.

"Good morning, Caitlin," I said. The pretty barista was working her own brand of magic with the espresso machine.

"Your drink will be right up."

"Thanks."

I turned away and a familiar figure caught my eye at a table in the back of the shop. Calybute Danforth owned the local newspaper, *The Buttermilk Bugle,* where my friend Clara Riley was now a fledgling reporter. My high school nemesis, Sassy Persimmons, worked there, too, selling ad space, which is how she and Clara became friends, much to my chagrin.

"Hey, Cal," I said.

Cal glanced up from the paper on the table and smiled. "Eden Fury. Clara told me you were back in town." Cal's family had a long history in Chipping Cheddar. The

Danforths were one of the founding families, along with the Davenports and Wentworths, to name a few.

"It was unexpected, but it's nice to be back among friends." I didn't mention family. The jury was still out on that one.

"Here's your vanilla latte, Eden," Caitlin said.

"Ooh, and a scone, too, please," I said. I returned to the counter to pay.

"Sure." Caitlin popped one of the scrumptious scones on a plate.

I swiped my card and then carried both items to join Cal at the small round table.

"I told Clara we should interview you about your involvement in catching Chief O'Neill's killer," Cal said. He was a slight, balding man with glasses and a pleasant smile. By all accounts, he was a decent boss—reasonable and kind.

"I thought Gasper covered the chief's death," I said. Gasper Cawdrey graduated from high school a few years ahead of me, although I didn't really know him.

"Of course," Cal said. "He's the senior reporter, but I promised Clara I'd try to assign her more than local sports. I'd like to make good on that promise."

"Well, it's hardly newsworthy that a federal agent apprehended a criminal," I said. "It's to be expected." As far as the human residents knew, I was an FBI agent in the cyber crime division and spent most of my time in an office catching online fraudsters and child pornographers.

"It's completely newsworthy," Cal insisted. "Chief O'Neill was immensely popular. People will want that closure."

"I don't think the Bureau will allow it," I said. "Classified information and all that." Especially when the killer was a fear demon that got sent back to Otherworld.

Cal smoothed the paper on the table. "Must've been exciting for you. I guess it's not typical that you get to see

7

action in the field when you're stuck behind a computer all day."

I blew the heat off my latte before venturing a sip. "I wasn't in the cyber crime division in San Francisco." I didn't care to elaborate, especially given the rumors that were already circulating about me.

"What made you decide to switch?" he asked. "Maybe thinking about getting married and settling down? Cyber crime is probably more conducive to family life."

As much as I disliked the implication that women needed to sideline themselves for the sake of a family, I understood that Cal came from a more traditional background. If he knew the truth about my job and my family, I doubt he'd know how to handle it. To be fair, most humans wouldn't, which is one of the reasons supernaturals remain hidden—some of us in plain sight.

A sudden burst of noise drew my attention to the front door. A young, slender redhead strode into the shop wearing dark sunglasses and a haughty expression.

"It's Mitsy Malone," a woman at the next table said.

I shot a quizzical look at Cal. "Who's Mitsy Malone?"

Even Cal appeared starstruck. "You don't know her? She's famous."

I wasn't someone who followed celebrities on social media. "What's she famous for?" And why was she in The Daily Grind in Chipping Cheddar?

Cal stared blankly in Mitsy's direction. "I have no idea, but aren't we lucky to have seen her?"

"Um, sure." I glanced over at Mitsy. The redhead was now encircled by a small group of customers, all clamoring for her attention. It seemed odd that a person as plugged in as Cal wouldn't know why Mitsy was famous. Maybe she was like a Kardashian. I'd have to ask Clara—or better yet—my sixteen-year-old cousin Meg. Mitsy looked about the same age as Meg, so my cousin was likely to have heard of her.

"I should have Gasper or Clara interview her," Cal said.

"Yeah, have her get to the bottom of why Mitsy's famous," I joked. "Anyway, it was nice catching up, but I need to get to the office."

"Nice to see you, too, Mitsy," he said, almost in a daze.

"Eden," I corrected him.

He didn't spare me a glance. "Yes, that's what I said."

I tossed my handbag over my shoulder and threaded my way through Mitsy's bevy of admirers. In the corner by the window, I recognized one of the local werewolves nursing a cup of coffee. Our eyes met and he lifted his brow as if to say *what the hell?* He seemed equally baffled by the attention Mitsy was receiving. I shrugged and pushed open to the door. It was time to get to work.

CHAPTER TWO

I STOOD in front of the door to my office, unable to get inside. My assistant Neville Wyman had been trying to beef up security ever since the fear demon that killed Chief O'Neill gained access to our office and removed a vital piece of evidence that would've led to his capture more quickly.

I pounded my fists on the door. "Neville, let me in!" The office was located on Asiago Street between a donut shop and a tattoo parlor. The location wasn't necessarily unsafe, but it wasn't somewhere I cared to linger on the sidewalk.

The door finally swung open and Neville stood in the doorway, red-faced. "Apologies. I must've overdone the ward." Neville was a talented wizard, but sometimes his enthusiasm got the better of him.

"You think?" I blew past him and tossed my handbag onto my desk. "So what's on the agenda today? Any demons to send packing to Otherworld?"

"Not today, o' kindly one." He cleared his throat. "I mean, Agent Fury."

"Eden," I reminded him. If Neville and I were going to work closely together, a first name basis seemed appropriate.

Fergus never called me Agent Fury. Sometimes he called me Garden Of and thought that was hilarious. He was such a nice guy that I always laughed politely.

"Holes is running a BOGO special today if you're interested," Neville said.

"Buy one get one free on donuts?" I queried. "That sounds dangerous."

Neville smiled. "It's good to be naughty on occasion."

"If your idea of naughty is two donuts instead of one, you go right ahead." I was accustomed to my family's idea of naughty, which usually meant a flagrant display of dark magic or vengeance.

"What's it like?" Neville asked.

I pulled a bottle of water out of my handbag and set it on the table. "What's what like?"

"Being a part of a family like yours," Neville said.

I turned to face him. "What do you mean?"

"Your father...He's a..."

"A vengeance demon. You can say it, Neville. I'm well aware."

"And your mother..."

"Likes her black magic as much as she likes Chanel No. 5 and kitten heels."

"And yet you became a federal agent," Neville said. "Fascinating."

"From the time I was old enough to express an opinion, my family said that I was drawn to the light. I shied away from hurting anyone and didn't want to use my magic." I laughed. "They tried their best to encourage me the other way, especially when they realized I was a fury."

"Furies do have the potential for tremendous power," Neville said. "I've taken the liberty of doing more research..."

I held up a hand. "Thanks, but I don't need tremendous power, Neville. I'm happy the way I am." I spun in a circle in

11

my chair, eager to lighten the discussion. I didn't like to talk about my family or my abilities. "So what did you and Paul do when there wasn't a supernatural criminal to hunt down?"

"Well, I often worked on new ideas for spells and such, and Paul would patrol the town, follow up on any reported incidents. He'd also keep track of new residents and drop in on any supernatural ones. And he performed regular checks on the portal."

"Why would he check on a dormant portal?" I asked.

"To make sure it's still dormant, of course."

My heart skipped a beat. "Is there actually a chance that could change?" I'd never heard of a portal reopening. It would mean chaos for the entire region until proper security could be put into place. The fallout would be catastrophic.

"It's not a huge concern, but it remains a possibility. The portal is still there, after all. Under the right circumstances, I suppose it could be reopened."

"Hmm. I haven't been to the portal," I said. "Maybe I should do that." On a regular basis. If there were any change in the portal's status, I'd want to be the first to know about it. As the lone FBM agent in town, I was the first line of defense.

"Before you go," Neville began. He quickly hesitated and bit his lip.

"What is it?" Whatever it was, he didn't look happy about it.

"Um, this came for you." He retrieved a letter from his desk and handed it to me.

"Do you always read the mail addressed to your boss?"

"Yes," he said. "As your assistant, it's considered part of my duties."

"I thought you were more inventions, less admin."

Neville straightened. "I'm both."

"What is it?" I scanned the contents. "They want me to *what?*" I leaned back in my chair. "Are they serious? How am I supposed to do this now?"

"Not now," Neville said. "Next month. Apparently, because you never trained with the Federal Bureau of Magic, only the FBI, the Bureau has decided to help you brush up on supernatural basics."

"I'm a fury for Hecate's sake," I said heatedly. "I don't need tips on how to be…myself."

"But you've never been a fury for the FBM," Neville said. "You told me yourself that you didn't use your powers as an FBI agent. You just told me, in fact, that you resist using them at all."

"That's because I don't want to." It wasn't just my family I wanted distance from—it was my true nature. The more I used my powers, the more likely I'd inherit more fury traits and eventually succumb to the dark side. Black wings were my latest gift from the gods and I desperately wanted the receipt so I could return them.

"It won't be forever," Neville said, attempting to comfort me. "The letter says it's a two-week intensive course with one of their best instructors."

"Terrific." I shoved the letter in the top drawer. I'd worry about it next month.

"One more thing, Agent Fury."

"Eden."

"One more thing, Eden." His cheeks turned crimson. "Apologies, that will take some getting used to." He searched his desk for another sheet of paper. "Ah, here it is."

I glanced down at the handwritten letter. "Who writes with a pen anymore?" And in such a loopy script?

"It's from Aggie Grace," he said. "She's the secretary of the supernatural council."

Aggie is also one of my neighbors. She lives with her two

sisters on Munster Close. The Graces were inherently good and I enjoyed spending time with them as a child, much to my family's dismay.

I squinted at the letter, trying to decipher the flowery writing. "I have to attend a meeting?"

"Paul was a member," Neville said. "The FBM agent in town has a permanent seat on the council. They expect you to take his place."

"Oh." I guess it made sense. "Can you read when it is? I can't understand Aggie's handwriting."

"Tonight at seven," Neville said. "In the private room at Chophouse."

"That's convenient. I'll see my cousin. Rafael's the chef and owner there."

Neville puckered his lips. "Ooh, that's an excellent establishment. I've taken my more serious dates there."

It hadn't occurred to me to ask Neville anything about his personal life. "You're not married?"

"No," he said. "I've tried a few of the dating sites, both human and supernatural, but no luck yet." He offered a rueful smile.

"Dating is overrated anyway," I said and vaulted from my chair. "If anyone calls, I'm checking the portal and making sure it's safe for humanity."

Neville saluted me. "Would you like me to bring you anything from Holes while you're gone? BOGO before they go go?"

"No donuts today, thanks. I already scarfed down a scone." And now I could go outside and walk off the calories. I was never one to be sedentary and I initially worried that this position would chain me to a desk for the rest of my career. A daily check of the portal would be good exercise.

The portal is located near the vortex, which is a place of powerful energy where multiple ley lines converge. Humans don't know about the portal or the vortex, of course. Supernaturals are drawn to it, though. For that reason alone, it was worth patrolling the area on a regular basis.

As I left the seedy side of town, the buildings became brighter and better maintained. Chipping Cheddar's picturesque downtown was a magnet for tourists. Between the waterfront overlooking the Chesapeake Bay and the river that cut straight through town, there were also plenty of parks and other outdoor spots to enjoy. And if your name was Beatrice Fury, you included the cemetery on that list.

I stopped in the middle of Pimento Plaza and let the warmth of the sun wash over me.

"I was wondering when I'd run into you again."

My skin crawled at the sound of my ex-boyfriend's voice. Tanner Hughes was the poster boy for 'don't judge a book by its cover.' The attractive cover lured you in, but the story inside was a disappointing mess.

"Hello, Tanner." I glanced at the statue of Arthur Davenport in the center of the plaza. "Isn't this where I ran into you last time?"

He grinned. "We'll consider it our special place."

My gag reflex kicked in. "We have to stop running into each other like this." Really.

Tanner inched forward. "We haven't properly caught up since you've been back."

"You're dating Sassy, the girl you cheated on me with in high school. You haven't proposed and she worries you never will. You both work in sales. Miraculously, your mother still thinks you walk on water." I crossed my arms over my chest. "Anything I've missed?"

Tanner wagged a finger. "I see someone's been asking around about me."

"See? We're all caught up now." I started forward to move past him, but he caught my arm.

"How about a drink tonight? We can reminisce."

"I'd rather tie myself to train tracks and wait for imminent death."

Tanner's grin turned wolfish. "Holy smokes, I've missed that feisty attitude."

I loosened his grip on my arm. "I've got somewhere to be, Tanner. You'll have to annoy me some other time."

He winked, as though we'd just shared a secret joke. "You got it, babe."

Blargh. I wanted a quick shower to wash away all traces of our contact. Too bad the bay wasn't warm enough for swimming yet.

I continued to the promenade and walked along the waterfront, admiring the view of the boats as I went. The sound of movement in the bushes reached my ears and I stopped short. I glanced around but saw nothing. As I took another step, I heard a muffled voice. My mind went straight to the recent murders in town. Although I'd caught the demon responsible, I was wary of another incident, so I dove straight through the bushes to confront my would-be attacker.

"What are your intentions here?" I demanded, as I burst into a small clearing. My jaw unhinged when I realized the scene I'd stumbled upon. A man and a woman were half-dressed and in the midst of an intense make out session. Based on the unopened containers of food on the blanket, their private picnic had quickly turned frisky. They jumped apart and gaped at me. Thankfully, I didn't recognize either one of them.

"I'm so sorry," I said. "I thought someone was stalking me."

The woman grabbed her shirt from the blanket and held it in front of her chest. "You nearly frightened me to death."

The man stared longingly at the woman. "And if that

had happened, I would take this knife and stab myself in the heart so that I could join you. I never want us to be apart."

The woman sighed dreamily. "Oh, Maxwell. You wouldn't."

"No, he wouldn't," I said, "because that's a butter knife." I inclined my head toward the dull blade on the blanket.

Maxwell pulled her into his arms and kissed her. "I've waited years to be with you. I won't let death come between us."

"Sorry for interrupting," I said, but they weren't listening.

I returned to the promenade and jogged along the path, past the lighthouse, until I reached the triangular stretch of land between the bay and the river. I felt a rush of energy as I passed the vortex.

The entrance to the portal wasn't visible to humans without the Sight. Residents referred to the hillside as 'the mound' and often used it as a geographical reference point.

I ducked my head and entered the mouth of the hill. This wasn't my first visit to the portal. As kids, my brother and I would dare each other to come here and tempt fate. He'd cajole me into standing in front of the portal and calling to inhabitants in Otherworld to come and get me. Then I'd run screaming from the hillside when my brother would make a sudden noise or jump out and grab me. Sometimes, I'd invite Clara to join us, but she never wanted to come here. As an empath, she wasn't comfortable with the powerful energy that emanated from Otherworld. It was probably for the best since my brother would've scared the daylights out of her anyway.

I scoured the hollow of the hill. Nothing seemed out of the ordinary. No unusual pulses of energy or evidence of tampering. Satisfied, I turned to leave. I wondered whether Paul kept a log of his visits. I'd have to check with Neville.

As I emerged from the shadow of the hill, I walked smack into the broad chest of Sawyer Fox, the new chief of police.

"Agent Fury?" Chief Fox gripped me by the shoulders to prevent me from stumbling backward. "I'm so sorry. I didn't see you there." He glanced around. "Where on earth did you come from?"

I struggled to form words, which seemed to be a common occurrence in the handsome chief's presence. "Out walking," I croaked. "Nice day."

"Yeah, we've been pretty lucky with the weather."

Sweet mother of lust, did he have to look so amazing? I wasn't generally a sucker for a guy in uniform, but sheesh. He wore it too well.

"What are you doing out here?" I asked, pulling myself together.

"Got a call for help down by the river," Chief Fox said. "Two brothers were fighting. You know how that goes. One of them tells the other one he hopes he breaks a leg or something to that effect." The chief chuckled. "Lo and behold, that's what happens."

"I bet the brother feels sorry about it now." I could only imagine what would've happened if the things Anton and I used to say to each other actually occurred. We'd both be dead by now.

"Oh, you bet he does. Rode in the back of the ambulance with him and everything."

"Guilt is a powerful motivator," I said.

"Love is an even stronger one," he replied.

We fell silent for a moment.

"I should get back to the office," I finally said.

"How's that lamp working out for you?"

I'd told the chief that my office lacked natural sunlight, so he'd bought me a sun lamp as a gift for capturing Chief O'Neill's killer. The new chief didn't know that a fear demon was responsible. He didn't know anything about supernaturals and I intended to keep it that way.

"It's wonderful, thank you." It really was.

"Want a ride back?" he asked. "My car's parked over there." He motioned toward the road.

My whole body warmed at the thought of being alone in a car with Chief Fox, but I knew I had to keep my distance. The chief was human and I...wasn't. It was too risky.

"No, thanks. It's a beautiful day and I need the exercise," I said.

"Well, I guess I'll see you around."

"It's a small town," I said. "It can hardly be avoided." I paused. "Not that I'd want to avoid it."

"I should hope not," he said. "People who want to avoid the police are often guilty of something."

The only thing I was guilty of right now was being a stammering moron.

"Nice running into you, Chief—literally," I said, and then hurried back toward the promenade before I could make an even bigger fool of myself.

CHAPTER THREE

THE SUPERNATURAL COUNCIL meeting was held in a small room at the back of Rafael's restaurant that was normally reserved for private parties. I didn't know very much about the council, other than its existence. I recognized Aggie Grace at the round table, along with Adele LeRoux, my grandmother's witchy rival. Adele's ancestors originally hailed from Louisiana and were one of the first black families to settle in Chipping Cheddar. Adele was now the matriarch of her magical family, which included a daughter, Rosalie, and a granddaughter closer to my age, Corinne. Although I liked Corinne, I'd kept my distance over the years due to the rivalry between our families.

"Eden Fury, what a delightful surprise." Adele scraped back her chair and crossed the room to offer me a kiss on each cheek. She wore a beautiful headscarf with a gold dress and tasteful jewelry. Adele had always outshone my grandmother in the fashion department, not that I'd ever admit it out loud. Disloyalty like that was grounds for a severe hex in my house.

"Good to see you, Mrs. LeRoux," I said. "You look

wonderful."

Adele returned to her seat. "Now don't go saying things you don't mean. I look old and tired because I am old and tired."

"Hush, Adele," Aggie interrupted. "You're as lovely as you've ever been. Your spirit shines ever so brightly." The grace shifted her attention to me. "Hello, neighbor. Why don't you join us, now that you're taking Paul's place?"

I took the seat beside Adele. "Good to see you, Aggie. I've been meaning to drop in and say hello."

Aggie waved a bony hand. "Don't worry about it, darling. I know you have your hands full. You stop in whenever it suits you. You know you're always welcome."

"Thanks," I said. "How are your sisters?"

"Well, you know Thalia and her gardening," Aggie said. "I swear she's outside in the morning when I get up and still there when I come home, no matter how late it is."

"And Charity?" I asked.

"Busy with nonprofits, as always. Her donations are way up this year. The internet has done wonders for fundraising."

"That's great." Charity worked as a consultant to organizations, helping them with fundraising and other cogs in the nonprofit wheel. "So who else is coming?"

The words barely left my lips when the door opened and Husbourne Crawley sauntered into the room. My other neighbor wore one of his signature pale linen suits complete with a straw hat. I once told Fergus that Husbourne reminded me of Foghorn Leghorn, the rooster from the cartoons. He laughed about that for a week straight.

"Look at this," Husbourne drawled. "A reunion. We could've done this pow-wow on Munster Close and saved ourselves a trip."

"I would not set foot on Munster Close, Husbourne," Adele said. "You know this."

"Grandma hasn't warded the street in years," I assured her. That I knew of, anyway.

"So glad you're a part of this Eden, sweetheart," Husbourne said. "Pidcock was a nice enough fella, but talking to him was like talking to a glass of tap water."

"Aren't you on the town council?" I asked him.

"Why, yes," Husbourne said. He took the seat adjacent to me. "We've always had one member that sits in on both council meetings. Helps to streamline information and cut down on the rumor mill."

I smiled at Husbourne. "You're like a double agent."

"I could say the same to you."

Rafael threw open the door and greeted us all with a wide smile. "Welcome, esteemed members of the council." His gaze alighted on me. "Splendid, Eden. I was hoping you'd be the replacement." He scrutinized the table. "And where is Mr. Phelps?"

"Monroe Phelps?" I asked. I remembered the Phelps family. Werewolves. One of the Phelps wolves used to babysit my cousin Julie when I wasn't available.

"Not Monroe," Rafael said. "His son, Hugh."

"I'm not late, am I?" Hugh Phelps swaggered into the room.

"Have a seat, son," Husbourne said. "We're just getting started."

"Would anyone like to order before you begin?" Rafael asked.

"The usual round of drinks, please," Adele said. "And the spinach and artichoke dip."

Aggie lit up at the mention of the appetizer. "I think we'll need two of those. That dish is inspired, Rafael."

He bowed slightly. "I am particularly proud of that one. One must not simply *chop* the artichoke hearts..."

Adele smiled. "We recognize your culinary genius, Rafael.

No need to get into specifics."

"Do I want the usual round of drinks?" I asked. I had no idea what the drink was.

"It's tradition," Adele said.

Rafael clapped his hands. "I will lock the door behind me and return shortly with your order." He looked at me. "Julie and Meg will be in the dining room shortly. Come and see them when you're finished."

"I will."

"It's so sweet of your cousin to wait on us personally," Aggie said, once Rafael left the room. "He takes excellent care of the council."

"It's in his best interest," Adele said. "He's a supernatural, too."

"I don't know about anyone else," Hugh began, "but I have a busy day tomorrow, so I suggest we get started."

I listened to Aggie read the minutes from the last meeting. There wasn't much to report. Some supernaturals had been a bit rattled by the recent murders and the appearance of the fear demon, but no one had acted out of line with supernatural ordinances. These rules weren't publicly available, of course, but every supernatural family in town had access to them. That way no one could claim ignorance.

"Mrs. Huntington is complaining about her flowerbeds again," Adele said.

Everyone groaned.

"Why does she complain to the council about her flowerbeds?" I asked.

"Because she insists the werewolves are watering her lawn, if you understand my meaning," Adele said.

"That woman is obsessed with her gardens," Husbourne said, exasperated.

"She is a gnome," Aggie pointed out.

Hugh shook his head. "No one is venturing anywhere

near Mrs. Huntington's flowerbeds. I checked it out myself the last time she filed a claim. The only animal I smelled there was a cat."

"Well, she does own three of them," Aggie said. "I imagine one of them is the culprit."

"She just has a thing against werewolves," Husbourne said. "I recall a few years back when she complained that a werewolf was mussing up her garbage cans. Turned out to be a raccoon."

"We don't want her calling the police station," Aggie said. "That would be a real headache for all of us."

"I'll speak to her," Adele offered. "She doesn't mind witches so much."

"Speaking of the police, what's the verdict on the new chief?" Husbourne asked. "Supers have been asking me, but I haven't had the privilege of meeting him myself yet."

"Eden, you worked with him during the investigation into Chief O'Neill's death," Adele said. "What do you think of him?"

"Well, I admired his technique." And his physique. And his sea-green eyes. "He seems to have a good head on his shoulders."

"And good shoulders, too, from what I hear," Adele said with a smirk. "My granddaughter is itching to get to know him better."

I tensed at the mention of Corinne's interest in the chief, which was silly. I barely knew him. Not to mention the fact that he was human and I was a vengeful fury in the making. It would be a mistake to get involved with him on anything more than a professional level. And I repeated this mantra to myself every time I found my mind wandering in his direction.

"He doesn't know that the real killer was a fear demon, does he?" Hugh asked.

"No, definitely not," I said. "Chief Fox will be as in the dark as Chief O'Neill was." What would he think of me if he ever knew the truth?

"What about news from the FBM?" Hugh asked. "Anything to report, Eden? Paul used to give us a mini-briefing every month."

"Nothing at the moment," I said. "The fear demon was returned to Otherworld. I've been getting up to speed on everything in the office and checked out the portal. Still dormant." I smiled and knocked on the table for luck.

Rafael entered the room with our round of drinks and the appetizers. I sniffed the glass of golden liquid that he set in front of me. It smelled sweet. "What is it?"

"It's called Fairy Dust," Aggie said. "An old recipe that I gave to Rafael some time ago. Closest we'll get to nectar. He doesn't keep it on the menu, but he's kind enough to serve it to us during our monthly meetings."

I swallowed a mouthful. "Delicious."

"Dig in," Adele said, gesturing to the plates of spinach and artichoke dip. "Nobody makes this like your cousin. He elevates it to an art form."

I was glad Rafael was using his talents for good, unlike certain members of my family.

"We do have one matter of a more serious nature to discuss," Husbourne said. He wore a solemn expression. "There are reports of a turning."

Aggie gasped. "A turning? Here in Chipping Cheddar?"

"Afraid so," Husbourne said.

"This sounds like my territory," I said. "Why hasn't the FBM been alerted?"

"Because the case hasn't been confirmed yet," Husbourne explained.

"How do we confirm it without an investigation?" I asked.

"The man doesn't seem to be any danger," Husbourne

said. "In fact, he's refused to leave his house."

"What about the one that turned him?" Hugh asked. "Seems to me that we've got a danger to the community right there."

"I'll speak to him," I said. "It should be my job anyway. What's his name?"

"William Hickes," Husbourne said. "Lives on Bleu Cheese Court. Number five."

"Thanks." I made a mental note to pay Mr. Hickes a visit tomorrow. If this really was a turning, then we had a very serious crime on our hands. Vampires living in this world were prohibited from turning anyone or drinking human blood straight from the tap. A violation meant a return to Otherworld or, even worse, the death penalty.

We finished our nibbles and drinks and chatted for a few more minutes about the state of the economy, the decent weather, and my return to town. I was relieved when the meeting finally adjourned because I didn't want to share the details of my transfer from the FBI. They didn't need to know that I'd siphoned powers from a vampire and had momentarily become one myself—nearly killing my partner in the process.

I left the private room to seek out Rafael's wife and sixteen-year-old daughter in the main dining area. From a table in the corner, Meg caught my eye and waved.

"How was your first meeting?" Julie asked. The werewolf had been a surprise choice of bride for Rafael, a dedicated warlock.

"I have my work cut out for me," I said vaguely. I didn't want to spread alarm over a possible turning. It was the kind of news best kept quiet.

"I'm glad you're on the council now," Julie said. "It'll be good to have a family member with their eyes and ears on supernatural affairs."

"It makes sense as part of my new job," I agreed.

"I bet your mom and grandma are happy," Julie whispered. "They've always hated that Adele was on the council."

I suppressed a smile. "Can you imagine one of them on the council, though? I can't imagine how many complaints they've triggered over the years." My family wasn't known for towing the line. It was a miracle my father managed to have a long-standing friendship with the chief of police.

"Between the FBM and the council, you're going to be a popular supernatural in town," Julie said. "You'll have your finger on the pulse of this community."

"Hey, that reminds me," I said, turning toward Meg. "Who's Mitsy Malone?"

Meg laughed. "You, too? I think the whole world knows her now."

"Now?" I queried. "Why, what did she do?"

"Nothing as far as I know," Meg said. "She has a YouTube channel, but she talks about books."

"And what's wrong with books?" Julie asked. "You love to read."

"I know," Meg replied. "I'm not knocking it, but how many YouTubers are famous for talking about books? It's weird."

"I don't know any famous YouTubers at all," Julie said. "So I don't understand it on any level."

"I'm surprised you'd know anyone on YouTube, Meg," I said. According to my mother, Meg was a teen hipster who eschewed social media and other mainstays of her generation.

"I have a computer at home," Meg said. "I use it…sometimes."

Julie elbowed me. "Tell her she needs a phone, Eden. Tell her about all the horrible monsters out there that you have to protect us from."

27

"Well, to be fair, it's only been one fear demon," I said.

"And what if the fear demon had attacked Meg?" Julie asked. "Without a phone, how would she have called for help?"

"Fear demons don't necessarily attack directly," I said. And a phone didn't help his three victims either.

Julie focused on her daughter. "What if you get kidnapped?"

"I'm sure he'll take my phone first," Meg replied. "Then you'll be out a daughter *and* an expensive phone."

Julie wasn't prepared to give up just yet. "What if you're lost?"

"Lost how? I don't drive yet."

"In the woods," Julie said.

"I'm a werewolf," Meg said. "How would I get lost in the woods?"

"I don't know." Julie waved a hand airily. "Maybe you'd go somewhere new so you could smoke cigarettes without getting caught."

"Gross." Meg wrinkled her nose. "I'd never ingest that garbage into my lungs."

"You need a phone," Julie insisted. "You won't have any friends. That's how they all communicate these days."

"Mom, stop with the fear-mongering!" Meg said. "You always envision the worst-case scenario for everything. I have friends. I live in a safe town. I have a computer at home. A phone isn't a necessity at this point in my life."

I had to admire Meg's fortitude.

"Maybe if you stop pushing, she'll eventually decide she wants a phone on her own." I knew how stubborn I could be at Meg's age. The harder my parents pushed, the deeper my toes dug in. Okay, that behavior may have continued all the way until...now.

"I bet Mitsy Malone has a phone," Julie said.

"She does and she's on it all the time," Meg said. "Everyone's always texting her, like her fame is going to rub off on them. It's not osmosis." She slumped in her chair. "I feel sorry for David."

"Who's David?" I asked.

"Her boyfriend," Meg said. "He's a really nice guy and they've been together for over a year."

"Why feel sorry for him?" Julie asked. "It's nice for the woman in a relationship to shine."

"I guess so," Meg said. "But the whole thing is odd. David does the YouTube channel with her, but her popularity has skyrocketed, yet no one pays him any more attention than they ever did."

"She *is* pretty," I said.

Meg shrugged. "She sure seems to like the attention. Even the teachers are favoring her. I heard she got out of writing her English essay because Ms. Hunt is such a fan."

"Well, it is a YouTube channel about books," Julie said diplomatically. She shifted her attention to me. "Was that Hugh Phelps I saw in the council meeting?"

"I figured you'd know him," I said. "I only remember his dad."

"His sister used to babysit me," Meg said. "Paisley."

"I don't remember either one of them from school," I admitted. The local high school wasn't huge, but there were enough kids that it was difficult to know and remember everyone.

"Hugh would've graduated before you started," Julie said. "Paisley was two years ahead of you, I think."

"She was a great babysitter," Meg said. "We bonded over the whole werewolf thing. She's very militant about shifting, though. Won't take a potion or anything to stop the change because it's natural."

"The whole family is like that," Julie added. "That's why

we never mixed with them socially very often. They also don't like that I married Rafael."

"They try to keep relationships within the pack?" I asked.

"There's not enough of a pack to support that attitude," Julie said. "If that's what they want, they should move to Otherworld where they won't be inbreeding."

"You never know, Meg," I said. "In a few more years, you might be Hugh's type."

Meg grimaced. "He's old."

I leveled a gaze at her. "Old or too old for you?"

"Fine, too old for me."

"I actually think Hugh is more open to dating other species," Julie said. "I've seen him here with dates and they've mostly been human."

"Like Kyle Radnor," Meg said. "He married a human."

"I wouldn't remind the pack of that fact right now," Julie said. "If gossip is to be believed, his wife is having an affair with another human."

"Does Kyle know?" I asked.

"I doubt it," Julie said. "He's a werewolf. If she provoked his jealous side, we'd know about it by now."

"Dad always says it's dangerous to become romantically involved with humans," Meg said. "That's why I plan to stay single forever."

"You won't always feel that way," Julie told her.

"I might," Meg replied. "Look at Eden."

"Eden will meet a nice young demon and settle down right here in Chipping Cheddar, won't you?" Julie patted my hand reassuringly.

I managed a weak smile. "From your lips to the gods' ears."

For once in my life, I really hoped the gods weren't listening.

CHAPTER FOUR

"CAN you believe John decided not to renovate the barn?" My mother's arms were cemented to her hips and she stared at me, as though I were somehow to blame.

"What happened?" I asked. "He seemed excited to take on the project."

"He's not a carpenter anymore," my mother said. She snapped her fingers. "Just like that! Apparently, he bought a boat and intends to live there while he writes a novel."

I frowned. "You're talking about John, the carpenter?"

"No, she's talking about John the Baptist," Grandma interjected. "Jesus was the carpenter."

"Thanks for the religion lesson, Grandma." I faced my mom. "I got the impression John enjoyed his work. Now he wants to write a book?"

"I was surprised, too, but I suppose this is what money does to a person," my mother huffed.

"Money? Did he get some kind of inheritance?" I asked.

Aunt Thora glanced up from her needlework. "No, dear. He won the lottery. The cashier at the grocery store told me. Everyone in town is talking about it."

"Wow." I'd never met anyone who'd actually won the lottery. "How much?"

"I heard a cool mill," Aunt Thora said.

Grandma squinted at her. "A cool mill? What are you—a gangster's moll?"

"Like you don't abbreviate words," Aunt Thora said in an accusatory tone.

"I abbreviate the *right* words," Grandma replied.

"Now he'll never date me," my mother complained. "He'll be too rich."

"Yes, *that's* why," Grandma said.

My mother balked. "What? You think a young stud like that can't be attracted to me?"

I closed my eyes. "Please don't use the word stud within earshot of me."

"Why are you closing your eyes?" Grandma asked. "Your ears are the issue."

"So do we have any other contenders for the barn?" I asked, because I was going to need to move out of this house soon if I intended to retain my sanity.

"I have a call in to Norm Capelli," my mother said. "He worked on the barn on the old Eaton property and it looks fabulous."

"What about Anton's contractor?" I asked. "The one who's remodeling his house?"

My mother's eyes bulged. "No, we can't do anything that would interfere with Anton's renovations."

"I second that," Grandma said. "These children are constantly underfoot. They need their own space."

I surveyed the kitchen. "There are no children here now." I knew Olivia was at school. "Where's Ryan?"

"Napping," my mother said.

Right. Ryan's naptime was usually when my father

decided to sneak his grandson out of the house for a play date.

"Let me know what Mr. Capelli says," I said.

"Where are you going?" my mother asked.

"I want to talk to Dad," I said.

"Tell him about the carpenter so I don't have to text him," my mother said.

I nodded and went out to the backyard to whistle for Princess Buttercup, my hellhound. To any humans without the Sight, she looked like a black and white Great Dane. I found her as a puppy, abandoned at the entrance to the underworld.

Princess Buttercup came bounding around the side of the house with a branch in her mouth. Part of the branch had disintegrated thanks to the hellhound's acidic slobber. She dropped what was left of the branch at my feet.

"I can't throw this," I told her. "It's falling to pieces."

The hellhound hung her head.

"I'm going to see my dad," I said. "Want to come?" I picked up a different branch and threw it toward my father's yard. I had a good arm—one of my supernatural qualities that I only tended to use in connection with fetch.

Princess Buttercup chased the branch and I crossed the yard to my father's house, where he lived with Sally, my step-mom. I would've moved in with my father until I got my own place, but Sally's a vampire with OCD tendencies and I knew she'd find another occupant difficult. I had no doubt she wiped down the door handles after each visit.

I entered through the backdoor and straight into the kitchen, where my father was opening and closing cabinet doors.

"Stanley, why would you leave your glasses in a cupboard?" Sally said.

"I wouldn't," my dad replied. "But I can't find them anywhere else."

Sally pinned her gaze on the hellhound. "I just washed the floors, Eden."

Princess Buttercup gave me a sorrowful look.

"Sorry," I said. I held open the door and the hellhound returned outside with the branch. I suspected she'd end up digging a hole in their yard for spite.

"Would you like a drink, darling?" Sally asked. She looked elegant with her golden blond hair cut just below her ears and her white pantsuit adorned with a shiny gold belt. A simple gold necklace completed the ensemble. She was the most glamorous suburban vampire I'd ever met.

"No drinks until I find my glasses," my father grumbled.

"Where do you remember having them last?" I asked. Before he could answer, I marched across the kitchen and plucked a pair of glasses from the counter next to the coffee machine. "Do you mean these?"

My father swiped the glasses from my hand and put them on. "How did you see those?"

"How did you not?" I shot back. "They were right there on the counter."

Sally shrugged. "I was focused on other things."

"Where's Ryan?" I asked.

"Now that I have my glasses, I can find him," my father said.

"Hardy har. Very funny."

My dad snorted. "He's on the floor in the living room. I only came in here to find my glasses."

I skirted the counter and saw my one-year-old nephew on the floor, playing with colored blocks. "Hey, Ryan."

The little boy turned and smiled when he saw me. I dropped to the floor and began making a tower of blocks. "Has he napped at all? His eyes look tired."

"He didn't want to sleep," my father said. "He wanted to play."

"Of course he'd prefer to play. He's only a year old. He doesn't know any better." I smoothed back his wispy layer of hair. "You have to stop stealing time with him when he should be asleep."

"Why? I used to do it with you all the time," my father said. "Your mother would put you down for a nap and disappear to a coven meeting or what-have-you and I'd come in and sit with you in the rocking chair."

"Why not do that during my awake time?" I asked.

"Between your mother, grandmother and great-aunt, someone was always hovering. I felt like I didn't get time alone with my daughter."

That actually seemed sweet. "And what did we do? Did you read me stories?"

"Sure did," my father said proudly. "Revenge For Dummies. Malevolent Rulers: A History. That was quality time for you and me."

"No Cinderella or Velveteen Rabbit?" I asked.

My dad grimaced. "Not on my watch. I used to let you siphon power from me, too, so you could get back at your brother for being mean to you."

My eyes bulged. "You had me siphon vengeance powers? I don't remember that."

"You'd sleep well after that." He chuckled. "It always drained you."

"I guess so," I said heatedly. "I was only little. I couldn't handle power like yours."

My father wriggled a finger at me. "Ah, but you did. I built up your strength."

I shook my head in disbelief. My father never ceased to amaze me. "Sally, have you heard anything about a possible turning?" I asked.

Sally snapped to attention. "A turning? You mean a vampire?"

"Yes. I need to go and see someone named William Hickes today. The unofficial story is that he was turned."

Sally clutched her necklace. "I can't imagine such a thing. In a place like Las Vegas, maybe. Certainly not here."

I cocked my head. "Why Las Vegas?"

"Oh, you know. People get drunk. They gamble. Before you know it, a vampire has convinced them that they really do want to live for eternity together."

"It's not like there's a quickie divorce option," I said. "You become a vampire and that's usually the end of the story. Why doesn't anyone stop them?"

"You have FBM agents there," Sally said. "But supernaturals get away with a lot in a place like Vegas." She wiped down the counter with a cloth. "Are you sure he's been turned? Maybe it's one of those cases where a human has gone psycho and only thinks he's a vampire."

"Could be," I said. "That's what I need to go and find out."

"I hope it's a psycho," Sally said. "We don't need any more vampires in this town. I can barely tolerate the ones we have now."

"Are you forgetting that *you're* a vampire?" I asked.

Sally patted her sleek hair. "There are different classes of vampire, just like in any group."

"I'll let you know which class William Hickes falls into once I meet him," I said, "so you know whether or not to invite him to brunch."

Sally smiled, displaying a set of pristine fangs. "I look forward to your update."

I pulled into the driveway of 5 Bleu Cheese Court and cut the engine. I sat in the car for a moment and stared at the quiet house. If William Hickes was a recently turned vampire, he was likely freaking out, unless he'd entered some sort of understanding with his sire. That happened sometimes, not quite like what Sally described in Vegas, though. It was a more thoughtful approach. Arrangements were made between parties invested in a relationship. They filed paperwork in Otherworld and went through the process there. Never here, though. Here was a criminal offense.

I approached the door and gave it a firm knock. No one answered.

"Mr. Hickes," I called. "Are you in there? My name is Eden Fury. I'd like to speak with you." I didn't want to identify myself as an agent at the outset and risk scaring him into silence.

Although I heard movement in the house, the door remained closed.

"William? I understand something scary may have happened to you and I'd like to talk to you about it. I promise nothing bad will happen." A risky promise, but one that had to be made. I needed to see him and assess the situation.

I counted to ten and used a simple unlocking spell that Grandma had taught me to open the door. As a teenager, I'd been forced to use it on a frequent basis to take back belongings that my brother had stolen from me. Anton had been a relentless thief, always taking the one precious item he knew would rattle me. It was a wonder we had any relationship at all now.

Slowly, I entered the house. "William? I'm not here to hurt you. Please come and talk to me."

There was silence until a voice said, "But what if I hurt you?"

"William, I'm a federal agent and I have a few defensive skills," I said. "It's unlikely you'd be able to hurt me." I didn't relish the idea of siphoning vampire power again so soon, but it would weaken William long enough that I could subdue him.

A young man emerged from the shadows. His face was gaunt and his eyes were bloodshot. "You're Eden Fury." His voice reflected the surprise on his face.

"Yes, I said that."

"You don't remember me? We went to elementary and middle school together," he said. "I'm Will."

I studied the sickly young man. "Right. I remember now. You had a pet rabbit."

"Miss Fluffernutter." He managed a smile and I noticed his fangs peeking out.

"Why didn't you go to our high school?"

"My family moved when my parents divorced," Will said. "I moved back here after college. I had such happy memories of this town growing up that I wanted to come back as soon as I could." He grunted. "I guess everything seemed better before their divorce."

"If it's any consolation, my parents divorced when we were in elementary school. They still live five hundred yards away from each other." And I'd never wanted to come back.

His eyes rounded. "My parents would've killed each other living that close."

"So, you want to tell me how you acquired the new enamel?" I gestured to his fangs.

He licked his chapped lips. I doubted he was eating or drinking enough of anything. His whole system was probably in turmoil.

"Can we sit in the study?" he asked. "It's darkest in there. The light bothers my eyes."

"You know you can venture out in daylight, right?" I asked. "The whole vampires-only- come-out-at-night thing is just a myth." I followed him into the darkened study and perched on the arm of the loveseat.

"Okay, cool," he said. "I wasn't sure." He sat in a wingback chair. "Why do you know about this stuff? I didn't even know vampires were real until I became one."

"Let's not worry about that right now," I said. "I'm more concerned about you and how this happened. Do you know who's responsible?"

Will blinked. "Someone did this to me?"

"Someone didn't?"

He flopped backward. "I don't know. I woke up like this two days ago."

"Two days ago? You just woke up with fangs and a thirst for blood?"

He nodded. "I thought it was a dream at first. My mouth felt odd so I touched my teeth and pricked my finger. I ran to look in the mirror."

"And then what?"

"I couldn't see anything. Then I threw up."

Right. "Will, have you had anything to eat or drink since then?"

He gave me a pathetic look. "No. I've tried water, but I can't keep it down. I feel nauseous constantly."

"Okay, I can help you with that." I immediately texted Sally to ask for spare bottles of blood and sent her the address. Thankfully, I'd already apprised her of the situation so she wouldn't need to ask questions.

"I've never felt so ill," Will said, clutching his stomach.

"I'm sorry, Will," I said. "It's the transition period. It can be very rough, but you'll get through it."

"I thought I was going insane," he said. "I waited to go outside the first night because I thought I'd burn up in sunlight."

"Why did you go outside at all?"

"I wanted to talk to someone," he said. "Show them my mouth and see if I was going nuts."

A human without the Sight would have definitely thought he was nuts. They can't see vampire attributes like fangs, not unless someone spelled them.

"Who did you talk to then?" I asked.

"One of my neighbors had just come home from a date," Will said. "He got out of his car and asked if I was okay. I showed him my mouth and asked if he saw fangs."

"And what did he say?"

"He said he did and then he told me to go back inside and stay there."

"What's the neighbor's name?"

"Truman Etheridge."

A-ha. That explained how Husbourne Crawley found out. The Etheridges are fae. Truman must have reported it to the council.

"I'm sorry it took so long for someone to come and see you," I said. "There shouldn't have been a delay."

"Am I stuck like this?" he asked.

"I'm not sure yet," I said, though I didn't see how he'd be able to undo a turning. "I need more information from you. Let's retrace your steps leading up your first morning as a vampire and see if we can piece it together. Did you go to any bars or meet up with someone for a drink?"

"I went to Holes for a donut and coffee," he said. "That Paige sure is nice. I wish she wasn't married to that loser, Shia."

"I haven't met Shia yet, but my office is right next door to Holes."

He frowned. "That doesn't seem like a great place for an office."

"I didn't choose it."

"After Holes, I went for a walk along the river. I didn't see anybody there. I like to go when it's quiet and peaceful. To think."

"About anything in particular?"

His expression clouded over. "No, nothing really."

I didn't need Quantico training to know that was a lie. "Did you used to go there with your parents as a kid?"

He brightened. "Oh, all the time. I loved playing outside as a kid."

So it was a happy place for him. Good memories.

"I used to pretend the mound was a mountain peak and I was a lost climber with nothing except my wits to survive."

I smiled. "You had quite the imagination."

"I would dig holes, use a bucket and a rope to get water from the old well, all sorts of stuff."

"Why not get water from the river?" I asked.

"Oh, it was contaminated and, if I drank from it, I risked disease." He chuckled. "I think it was cholera. Anything to make my predicament more harrowing."

"Sounds like your parents didn't ever need to entertain you."

Will sighed gently. "Definitely not. I could play there for hours, perfectly content. My parents would have to drag me home."

The doorbell rang. "That's my stepmom," I said. "She's a vampire, too."

Will huddled in the chair and hugged a pillow. "A real vampire?"

I offered a reassuring smile. "Yes, Will. A real vampire like you." I went to the door and let Sally in.

"Doesn't she have to be invited?" Will called from another room.

"No," we yelled in unison.

Sally gave me a bottle of blood and I brought it into the room for Will. "You have a lot to learn," I said. "This is my stepmom, Sally Fury. She can answer any questions you might have."

Sally stood in the doorway. "Take slow sips. The last thing you want is a bright red stain on that light carpet."

Will stared at her. "Stains are the least of my concerns right now."

Sally squeezed my shoulder. "Why don't you let me take it from here, Eden? You go file a report or whatever it is you need to do."

"I don't want to file a report until I know more," I said.

Will's eyes widened. "Why would you file a report? Who are you?"

"I'm an agent for the Federal Bureau of Magic," I said. I needed Will to know he could trust me and that meant trusting him with my secret. "It's a secret division of the FBI. I handle supernatural occurrences in this jurisdiction."

"And I'm a supernatural occurrence?" he asked.

I gave him a sympathetic look. "I think you qualify."

"What happens to me if you file a report?"

"Don't worry, Will," I said. "We're going to keep this under wraps until I get more information."

He took a sip of the blood and his body relaxed. "Wow. I thought it would be disgusting."

Sally patted her bag. "There's more where that came from. I have both still and sparkling, once you've settled."

"Have you always been a supernatural?" Will asked me. "You seemed normal to me in school."

"I am normal," I said.

Sally rolled her eyes. "Except the way you bend your fingers. That's unnatural."

"I'm double-jointed," I huffed. "And I'm a fury, so my supernatural abilities aren't as obvious as, say, a werewolf."

Will recoiled. "Werewolves are real?"

"Basically, if you can imagine it, it exists," I said.

"Topless mermaids?" he asked.

"Right in the bay," I said. "You wouldn't have been able to see them before, but you can see them as a vampire."

Will was rendered speechless. "Is the whole world like this?"

"We're everywhere, but we gravitate to some places more than others." I didn't want to explain the portals. Will had enough information to process. "I'll leave you my number. Text me if you need anything and I'll be in touch."

"Thanks, Eden," he said. He took another sip of blood and a drop began to fall toward the carpet. Sally used her vampire reflexes to catch the droplet before it hit the carpet.

"Good luck, Will, but you don't need it," I said. "I'm leaving you in good hands."

Will gaped at Sally, awestruck. "I can see that." He shook his head. "I feel like I have so much to learn."

And so did I—like how in Hecate's name did Will Hickes become a vampire?

CHAPTER FIVE

I LEFT Will's and went back to the office to update Neville on recent developments. He gave me a list of local vampires so that I could start questioning them about Will. Even if they weren't the responsible party, they might have heard something. Vampires are notorious gossips. The next time I looked at the time, it was six o'clock and my stomach was rumbling. Neville had been gone an hour, so I headed home to take care of my appetite.

I sensed a bustle of activity the moment I stepped through the door and went into the kitchen to investigate. My mother took one look at me and raised her brow in silent criticism.

"What?" I asked. I glanced down at my jeans and T-shirt. The white shirt had an image of four foxes with 'sake' written below.

"At least wear a shirt that's grammatically correct," Grandma said. She stood at the stovetop, stirring a pot. "It technically says four foxes sake, not four fox sake."

I inclined my head toward the pot. "I see you do that physically as well as metaphorically."

My mother moved to stand between us. "Why don't you go wash up?" she said to me. "We're having dinner promptly at six-thirty."

"Why promptly?" Thanks to different schedules, our family tended to have a staggered approach to mealtimes.

"I took the liberty of inviting an old friend," my mother said.

It was then I noticed her sapphire necklace and matching earrings. And her perfectly coiffed hair. "Which old friend?"

"Hugh Phelps." Despite her best effort to murmur his name, I heard her loud and clear.

"How is Hugh Phelps an old friend?" I demanded.

My mother turned to busy herself with a cheese plate on the island. "We've known the Phelps family for generations."

"Monroe, maybe," I said. "Even his daughter." Whose name I forgot yet again. "I don't even remember Hugh. I was only reminded because of the council meeting."

"He's hard to forget now," Grandma interjected. "Even his muscles have muscles."

"I know what you're doing and it won't work." I spun around toward the attic. "Enjoy dinner. I'll be upstairs."

"Eden Joy Fury, you will clean up and report back here immediately," my mother said firmly. I felt the energy in the room change.

"Don't you dare cast a spell on me," I yelled over my shoulder.

Too late. I felt the magic attack my body and turn me back toward the kitchen.

"Stop," I said through clenched teeth.

My mother gave me a smug look. "What are you going to do—arrest me?"

"I might," I ground out. "Now stop the spell."

My mother folded her arms. "Not until you agree to clean up and come to dinner."

"I also invited someone," Aunt Thora said quietly. "Ted O'Neill. Would you be willing to come for him?"

I couldn't move my body, but my eyes darted in Aunt Thora's direction. Ted O'Neill is Chief O'Neill's brother and works at the lighthouse. He and Aunt Thora had been involved when they were much younger, but the family had warned my great-aunt against a relationship with a human. I'd visited Ted recently to break the news of his brother's death and had seen how lonely he was. Of course I would come for him. I wasn't a monster.

"Yes," I said, barely able to move my lips.

My mother flicked a finger and released me from her hold.

I bent my neck from side to side. "Don't do that again."

"It's my house, my rules," my mother said.

"You can't inflict magic on someone just because they don't do what you want," I said.

"Why not?" she replied. "I've been doing it your whole life."

No kidding. I didn't even need a curfew in high school. When the clock struck eleven, my mother's spell would drag me home no matter where I was. Clara understood when it happened, but I'd had to make up a variety of strange excuses when it happened with Tanner. One minute we'd be making out in his car and the next minute I'd be gone. Luckily, he wasn't the sharpest pine needle in the forest.

"You'd better be nice to Ted," I warned.

My mother and grandmother wore their best blank expressions.

"I don't know why you think I wouldn't." My mother wandered over to the sink and began loading dirty dishes into the dishwasher.

"It's not you I'm most worried about." I pinned Grandma

with a hard stare. "Ted is vulnerable right now. He needs kindness."

"And I'm sure my sister will give him all the kindness he needs…after dinner." Grandma turned back to her pot and continued to stir.

"You can go change your clothes now, Eden," my mother said. "You can't wear that outfit to dinner when you've had it on all day."

"That's what happens with clothes," I said. "You wear them until you get your shower and then pajamas."

"Not when someone special is coming to dinner," she insisted. "Great Nyx, it's no wonder you're still single."

"Hugh is a werewolf," I said. "Since when do you encourage relationships with shifters?"

"Since your cousin Rafael married Julie, that's when."

I couldn't argue with that. Julie had become a welcome addition to the family and we all fussed over Meg from the moment she was born.

"If you think Hugh is such a catch, why don't you put yourself in the running?" I asked. "You don't shy away from younger men."

My mother lifted her chin a fraction. "I just might, Eden, dear, but you're the one who needs to get a move on. My biological clock has self-destructed."

"Go on and change, Eden," my great-aunt encouraged. "Ted will feel the negative energy in the room if we keep this up. I need to calm the vibes." She shuffled over to the pantry and removed fresh sage from a jar. "Let's all be on our best behavior for his sake."

"Fine," I huffed. I hurried to the attic to change my outfit, but I deliberately chose the most boring clothes imaginable. Black jeans and a dull gray T-shirt. Drab didn't begin to describe the way I looked. I ran a brush through my hair, but only because I wasn't completely without vanity.

By the time I returned to the kitchen, our first guest had arrived. Hugh stood between the kitchen and family room with a beer in his hand. He was chatting amiably with Verity and Anton. His face lit up when he saw me.

"Fancy seeing you here," he said.

"I live here," I replied.

My mother shot me a dark look.

"I live in the attic," I added, just to annoy her more.

Hugh smiled. "Cool. I love attics. Maybe you can show it to me later."

Princess Buttercup rushed into the room and nudged me for attention. Hugh's eyes popped at the sight of her.

"A hellhound? Here?" The werewolf seemed taken aback. I half expected Princess Buttercup to growl at him, but she didn't seem bothered by his presence. That spoke volumes, to be honest. She was quick to tell me when she disliked someone and I trusted her judgment.

"She's a rescue," I explained. "But we're expecting a human guest, so no more talk of hellhounds."

Hugh grimaced. "Oh, sorry. I didn't realize."

On cue, the doorbell rang and Princess Buttercup raced to the door. She narrowly avoided tripping over Charlemagne, who slithered to the door as well. Candy stayed on the windowsill in the kitchen, not remotely concerned with the latest guest. My grandmother's black cat marched to the beat of her own drum.

A moment later, Aunt Thora appeared with Ted. His face was ashen as he observed the Great Dane and the python that entered the room ahead of him.

"Such interesting pets," Ted said.

"Scram, you two. You're making our guest uncomfortable." My mother shooed Princess Buttercup and Charlemagne down the hall and then turned to greet Ted with a blinding smile. "Welcome, Ted. It's been far too long. Can I offer you a cold drink?"

"We have fresh lemonade," Aunt Thora offered.

"Of course you do." Ted smiled at my great-aunt. "I'd be a fool to turn down your homemade lemons. It's a marvel you can grow lemon trees in this climate at all. Must be your magical touch, Thora."

"Must be." Aunt Thora smiled demurely before going to pour him a glass of lemonade.

My mother steered Ted into the open-plan room where the rest of us had congregated.

"Ted, do you know Hugh Phelps?" I asked.

"You're the lighthouse man," Hugh said, and shook the older man's hand.

"That I am," Ted said, puffing out his skeletal chest. "Best view in town."

"I'll bet," Hugh said. "I'd love to come up and see it sometime."

Ted beamed. "I wouldn't mind the company. Come whenever you like."

If one good thing came out of this dinner, it would be Ted reconnecting with people. I felt like he needed it more than ever, now that his brother was dead. I hadn't seen Chief O'Neill's ghost since the fear demon was apprehended, so I could only assume that he crossed over and was finally at peace. That was my hope anyway.

We chatted amiably for another twenty minutes with Hugh complimenting everything from my mother's choice in fragrances to the window treatments. He was liberal with his flattery, which only made me wary of him. I didn't trust anyone with that many compliments to dole out. On the other hand, Princess Buttercup had come into the room and settled at his feet. Maybe she just liked the smell of wolf, but I doubted it.

The rest of the family emerged from their rooms just before dinner was served. It was definitely a full house. My mother made sure to squeeze me between Hugh and Anton at the table.

"Well, this is cozy," Hugh said, grinning at me.

"Anton, would you mind scooting your chair over?" I asked. "Hugh needs more room."

"I wasn't complaining," Hugh said.

Olivia fixed her solemn gaze on me. "Is it true that you killed someone in California? Is that why you had to come back here?"

"Where did you hear that, sweetheart?" Verity asked.

I stiffened. "I didn't kill anyone." Fergus had needed a blood transfusion, but he was otherwise fine.

"Katie's mom told Andrea's mom that they made you change jobs because you killed someone," Olivia said.

"Well, it isn't true," I said. My face was warm so I knew my cheeks had to be blazing red. One of the disadvantages of pale skin was displaying my embarrassment for all to see.

"That's disappointing," Grandma mumbled.

I tried to reach her foot under the table with my own, but she was too far away. It was probably for the best. If I kicked her in the shin, she'd probably hex me right in front of Ted. As I moved my foot back to its place, I noticed Charlemagne slithering in and out of the chair legs.

"Charlemagne, no begging at the table," Verity said in a firm voice.

Candy jumped down from the windowsill and landed in front of the python, blocking his path. The snake opened his mouth and hissed and Candy responded in kind.

"Will you look at those two?" Grandma said. "I haven't seen two animals that infatuated since Hugh's parents started dating."

I cleared my throat loudly and jerked my head toward Ted.

"We're all animals, Eden," Ted said. "It isn't an insult."

Hugh nodded. "They still have a wonderful relationship."

"One you aspire to emulate, I imagine," my mother said.

Inwardly, I groaned. She was as subtle as a minotaur in a china shop.

"Most definitely," Hugh said. "Just waiting to find the right woman to share my life with."

The black cat swished her tail across Charlemagne's head and trotted back to her place on the windowsill.

"Eden doesn't have the same high bar, so there's less pressure," Grandma said. "Her parents can't stand each other."

My mother pressed her lips together and I stifled a laugh. It was petty, but I kind of loved when they turned on each other because it meant I was free and clear—at least for the moment.

"I wouldn't trade married life for anything," Anton chimed in. Someone was eager to score points with his wife. I wondered what he was trying to atone for.

"Eden, why don't you tell Hugh about your job in San Francisco?" my mother said. "Eden was an FBI agent, you know."

"Yes, same as here," I said pointedly.

My mother's gaze shifted to Ted and she flashed a dazzling smile. "Yes, of course, but in a different division."

"That sounds fascinating," Hugh said. "I like a woman who relishes action and adventure."

"Well, you won't find much of that here in Chipping Cheddar, I'm afraid," Ted said. "It's relatively quiet. Mick used to say that the worst crime we have here is petty theft, until he was murdered that is."

The table fell silent.

"I throw up when I drink orange juice," Olivia said, breaking the tension. "I hate pulp."

"Olivia, you shouldn't talk about such things at the table," Verity said. "It isn't polite."

"Why not?" Olivia asked. "Everybody throws up, just like everybody poops." She giggled at her own statement. "That's the best book."

"It is one of her favorites," Anton said.

Verity shot an annoyed look at her husband. "Please don't encourage her."

"Poop," Ryan said. He smashed his fist into his applesauce and laughed.

"That's not poop," Olivia said. "That's diarrhea."

I closed my eyes and tried to mentally teleport to my happy place, which was basically anywhere but here.

"Your children are charming," Hugh said.

"Charming?" Grandma repeated. "If you think that's charming, I have a few friends in the nursing home I can introduce you to."

Hugh chuckled. "I'd be delighted to meet them."

The rest of the meal continued in the same vein, with Hugh managing to catch every throw. I could tell it was grating on Grandma. She wanted to see his imperfections and he was refusing to bend under pressure.

After the apple pies were obliterated, Ted and Aunt Thora took a turn in the garden out back while Hugh thanked my family for a lovely evening.

"Early to bed, early to rise," he said. "I like to keep to my schedule."

"Eden will walk you out," my mother said. "Thank you so much for coming. It's been delightful."

"It certainly has," Hugh replied. Hugh offered his arm to me. "Shall we?"

I looped my arm through his.

"Don't rush back," my mother said. "We'll clean up."

"And by 'we,' you must mean you and the garden gnomes," Grandma said. "Because my arthritis prevents me from any type of cleanup activity."

"I'm sure there's a potion for that," I said.

Hugh and I made it as far as the front porch before he turned to me. "You're not actually interested in me, are you?"

I released his arm. "Uh, not really. Why?"

He dropped onto the porch swing. "The truth is I'm waiting for someone."

"Oh?" I moved to sit beside him. "Anyone I know?"

"I don't even know who she is yet," he said. "I ordered her."

I choked. "You *ordered* her? Like off a menu?"

He grinned. "Not quite. I used a matchmaking service that specializes in werewolf packs. She's basically a mail order bride."

Wow. I was not expecting that revelation.

"I thought you dated other species," I said.

"I do, but I have no intention of marrying any of them," Hugh said. "My family has been pressuring me to settle down and start producing pups, so I finally bit the bullet." He paused. "Not the silver one, of course."

"I guess it doesn't surprise me," I said. "Your family has always been old school when it comes to werewolf life."

He looked at me. "You mean the fact that we choose to turn?"

"Yes, and the fact you're only willing to marry another werewolf."

Hugh stretched his muscular arms over his head. "I would've been willing to entertain the idea of another species if I'd met a woman who made my fur curl, but I haven't."

"So you may as well toe the line?"

"Friction in the family is the worst," he said.

I laughed. "Trust me, I know." Then again, I wasn't willing to cave. I guess I was more stubborn than Hugh.

"Anyway, I just wanted to clear the air and make sure there were no hard feelings," Hugh said. "If we're going to serve on the council together, it would be nice to get along."

"We're totally good. No worries on my end." I couldn't speak for my mother, though. "Basically, if Princess Buttercup likes you, you've passed the Litmus test."

He rose to his feet and extended a hand. "To the start of a beautiful friendship, Miss Fury." He cleared his throat. "Excuse me, I mean Agent Fury."

"Just Eden is fine. See you at the next council meeting." I accepted his hand and shook it.

CHAPTER SIX

THE NEXT MORNING I sat with Sally in my father's house and reviewed the list of vampires in town. I figured that Sally knew most of them and could help me prioritize the order of interviews.

"I appreciate your help with this," I said. "I'm out of touch with the vampire community here."

"So am I, for the most part," Sally said. "They're not fans of your father."

"Because he's a vengeance demon and not a vampire?"

"No, because he's annoying." She offered a tight smile. "You know how loud your father can be. He doesn't know how to read a room."

I was familiar with my father's social graces, or lack thereof.

"So which vampire should we start with?" I asked.

Sally leaned over to consult the list. "We should see Bianca Mortimer first."

"We?"

"Bianca will be more forthcoming if I'm with you," Sally

said. "You know how insular the vampire community can be."

"You think she's the most likely to know something about Will? Doesn't she work in a salon?" I vaguely remembered her from visits to Scissors.

"Now she owns a salon that caters to supernaturals," Sally replied. "Everybody talks there. Sometimes, if I don't feel like reading or watching a film, I'll make an appointment at the salon and soak up the drama there."

"I hope they're mindful of their human customers," I said.

"Oh, Bianca has it glamoured to make it less appealing to humans," Sally said. "Looks like it belongs at the far end of Asiago Street. Humans don't set foot in there unless they're lost or desperate."

The salon sounded like a promising source of intel. "I don't have to get my hair done, do I?"

"I'll book us for pedicures with Bianca." Sally cast me a sidelong glance. "Though it wouldn't kill you to get a trim."

I rolled my eyes. "Now you sound like Mom."

Sally's jaw tensed. "I'll pretend you didn't just say that."

I handed her my phone. "Would you call from mine so I have the number?"

"Of course." Sally called and made the appointment. "We have thirty minutes. Plenty of time."

"We're lucky Bianca could fit us in."

Sally's lips curved into a smile. "Luck has nothing to do with it, darling. One of the perks of being married to a vengeance demon." She stood. "I'll go grab my sandals. I hate when I mess the polish the second I put my shoes on."

Twenty-five minutes later, we were on a side street downtown.

"Turn right here," Sally said.

I turned and noticed the sign for Sparkle up ahead. Part

of me wanted to view it through human eyes, just to see how unappealing it looked to them.

I nabbed the first available spot, showing off my parallel parking skills.

"You're so good at that now," Sally said. "I remember when you would end up a foot from the curb."

"I had a lot of practice in San Francisco," I said.

Sally opened her door. "I've been meaning to tell you... I'm sorry things didn't work out the way you hoped. I know you would've been perfectly happy to stay out west."

"Thanks, Sally. I appreciate that."

"Your father is over the moon, though," she said. "He's missed you."

"You mean he's missed trying to mold me into something I'm not."

"Now don't be so hard on him," Sally said. "His intentions aren't all bad."

"Maybe not toward me," I said. "I can't speak for the thousands he's pursued in the name of revenge."

Sally didn't respond. We entered the salon and were greeted by a young guy at the receptionist desk with a pierced nose and blue hair.

"Welcome back, Sally," he said.

"Good morning, Erik," Sally said. "We both have pedicures scheduled with Bianca."

"Are you sure you don't want me to bring in a second nail technician?" Erik asked. "It'll take longer if Bianca does both of you."

"We're not in any hurry," Sally said. She strode past the reception desk and I followed. My stepmom knew how to command a room. Every head swiveled in her direction as we passed by. No wonder my father had refused to leave Otherworld without her.

We entered a room labeled 'suite,' where a willowy brunette was filling up the footbaths.

"Good morning, Bianca," Sally said.

"Sally, my sweet." Bianca walked forward and kissed Sally on each cheek. "You haven't aged a day."

They both burst into laughter. Ah, vampire humor.

"Eden, you're so grown up," Bianca said, looking me up and down. "I remember when you were this scrawny kid who didn't want anything girly. No polish. No makeup. And now look at you." Bianca clucked her tongue. "You haven't changed a bit."

"I wear chapstick," I said defensively. "I hate dry lips."

Bianca motioned for us to sit. "What's the special occasion? A welcome home for Eden?"

"You know Eden is the new FBM agent in town," Sally said. She sat first and I took the seat beside hers.

"I heard all about it," Bianca said. "Congratulations, Eden. Your family must be very…" She hesitated, likely realizing that 'proud' wouldn't be the right word. "Very happy to have you home."

"They're adjusting," I said. "We all are." I slipped off my shoes and Bianca recoiled slightly. "My, what unexpectedly large feet for your slender frame."

"Eden's an anomaly in so many ways," Sally said. My stepmom's feet were, of course, perfect. Even her toes were easy on the eyes. With wispy hair and misshapen toes, my feet looked like they'd been inherited from Hobbits and then hexed by my family.

"Have you chosen a polish?" Bianca asked.

"She'd like my usual," Sally replied.

"I thought so." Bianca produced a bottle of crimson polish from her smock and placed it on the stand between our chairs. "Who'd like to go first?"

"Eden's needs are more urgent," Sally said.

Bianca digested the scene in front of her, clearly judging it the salon equivalent of a car wreck. "I agree." She plunged my feet into the water and began to scrub them. I tried not to react to the almost painful tickle.

"Any good gossip?" Sally asked. "Eden's been wanting to catch up now that she's back in town."

"I would think her mother and grandmother are up to the task," Bianca said, and I heard the trace of bitterness in her voice. No doubt my family had wronged her in some capacity in the past. That was their way.

"Vampire gossip, specifically," Sally said.

Bianca's head jerked up to look at me. "Is this because of your new job? You need to keep tabs on us? Paul Pidcock never did that."

"No, it's not like that," I said. "Do you know a young man called Will Hickes?"

Bianca looked blank. "Will Hickes? I don't think so. He's a vampire?"

"He is now," I said.

Bianca halted. "What do you mean—now?"

"I mean that he was a regular human and now he's not."

She met my inquisitive gaze. "Unholy hell, are you serious?"

I nodded. "He didn't know anything about supernaturals until he woke up as a vampire."

Bianca's jaw unhinged. "He literally woke up one morning and was a vampire?"

"I went to school with him, so I know he wasn't one before."

Bianca shifted her attention to Sally. "I guess you don't know anything?"

"Only what Eden's told me," Sally said. "I had to go to his house with emergency blood. Poor young man was so confused and understandably terrified."

"I'll swear on the deed to my salon, Eden," Bianca said. "I don't know anything about a turning." She seemed genuinely pained to hear about Will's situation.

"Have you heard of any vampires causing problems recently?" I asked. "Anyone resisting the rules?"

Bianca flinched.

"I'm not here to make trouble for vampires," I said, "but if someone is turning humans, it's a problem for everyone in Chipping Cheddar."

Bianca nodded. "There is one. He's a relative newcomer."

Why didn't that surprise me? Longtime residents were much more likely to keep up the charade. They wanted to be able to live here in peace.

"Do you mean Rupert?" Sally asked.

"That's the one." Bianca moved my feet out of the water and drained the footbath. She towel dried my feet and set to work on my cuticles.

"Who's Rupert?" I asked.

"He moved here from Otherworld about two years ago," Sally said. "He was attracted to the mystical energy, of course."

"He considered staying in New York," Bianca added. "That's the portal he came through to get here. He said he felt compelled to go south and ended up here."

"What makes you think he's trouble?" I asked.

"He's been challenging at times," Bianca said. "He's from an old vampire family in Otherworld, practically royalty, so he thinks he's above our laws here. Doesn't want to drink synthetic blood. Wants to tell women the truth about being a vampire. Thinks it's an aphrodisiac."

"He sounds like a threat to the community," I said.

"And with a new chief of police, the risk is greater than ever," Sally chimed in. "We can't be too careful."

"How is the new chief?" Bianca asked. "One of the stylists

said she saw him in Holes and that he's absolutely scrumptious."

I shifted in my seat, unwilling to answer.

"He has a gorgeous face," Sally said. "And his body—well, don't get me started."

"Bite, kill, or turn?" Bianca asked.

"Oh, honey, all three."

My face warmed. "Sally!" I didn't want to hear my stepmom talk about anyone like that, not even my dad.

"Sorry, darling," Sally said. "But it's true."

"How about you, Eden?" Bianca said. "Bite, kill, or turn?"

I bristled. "I'm not a vampire."

Sally patted my arm. "Sometimes it's good to pull the wand out of your bottom."

"And replace it with the chief's…"

I didn't let Bianca finish. "So where can I find Rupert?"

Bianca unscrewed the lid to the polish and began applying the deep red color to my toes. "Evergreen."

"Evergreen, the old mansion?" I asked.

"That's right," Bianca said. "He bought it and renovated it. I'm told he's using it for both personal and professional purposes."

"What professional purposes?" I asked. "Like a home office?"

Bianca snickered. "Something like that."

"Apparently, he's using the downstairs as a private club," Sally said. "He invites attractive women by special invitation only."

"What happens at the club? Gambling?"

"No idea," Sally said. "With Rupert, I can safely say I don't want to know."

"If you want to catch him off-guard, I'd suggest going after ten," Bianca said. "He'll be preoccupied with his…guests."

And more likely to answer my questions. Perfect. "Thanks, Bianca. You've been really helpful."

"No problem." Bianca slid her stool over in front of Sally's footbath. "Your turn, Mrs. Fury."

Even though Sally and my dad had been married for years, it still sounded strange to hear someone other than my mother referred to as Mrs. Fury.

While Bianca finished Sally's pedicure, I texted Neville to check whether there was a file on Rupert. The more I knew about him, the better.

"Who are you texting, Eden?" Sally asked.

"My assistant, Neville," I said. "He's going to pull Rupert's file if there is one."

"Is Neville single?" Bianca asked, with a knowing look at Sally.

"He's nice, but he's not my type," I said. Why did everyone seem so eager for me to have a love life? I was only twenty-six, not seventy-six. I had plenty of time.

"I would think nice is exactly your type," Bianca replied.

Sally slipped her dry toes into her sandals. "Let's leave Eden be. She gets enough pressure from her mother as it is."

I shot my stepmom a grateful look.

"Pressure is what makes a diamond," Bianca pointed out.

"Then I'd rather be a decaying carbon-based life form," I said.

Bianca's gaze traveled to the floor where I stood. "Honey, with those feet, it looks like you already are."

Sally and I arrived back at the house and my stepmom headed straight upstairs to use the bathroom. She tended to avoid public restrooms. When I was younger, I'd assumed it was a vampire thing. I only later discovered it was specific to Sally.

I wandered into the living room where my father was looming over his grandson.

"Come on, Ryan. You can spell it," he said. "It's only four letters."

"R-y-a-n," I said.

My father's brow wrinkled. "Not Ryan. Evil. E-v-i-l."

Of course. How silly of me.

"Stand up straight, Eden," my father said. "You're hunching again."

"I'm not hunching." Despite my protest, I squared my shoulders and sucked in my stomach. My father had served as the main critic of my posture since the day my spine was formed.

"How was the salon? It's nice to see you and Sally spending time together."

"She was really helpful today."

"Good. Now how about you help me? I can't find my glasses again." He scratched his head, looking perplexed.

"You're kidding, right?"

"No. I'm worried I left them at the country club."

I plucked the glasses from the coffee table in the middle of the room. "You mean these?"

My father's mouth opened and closed like a fish. "I don't understand."

"Maybe your vision is worse than you think," I said. "Why don't you make an appointment with the eye doctor?"

My father put on his glasses. "Maybe I will." He stared at the coffee table, frowning. "But I swear I checked the coffee table." He exhaled loudly. "I don't know what's going on with me. Sally thinks it might be early onset dementia."

Sweet Hecate. A vengeance demon with dementia? That could be dangerous for everyone.

Ryan giggled and I glanced over to see him swaying on his feet. He didn't have the standing thing down pat yet.

"Be careful." I rushed forward before he toppled over. I scooped him up in my arms and he smiled at me.

"Eye," Ryan said, and pushed his finger into my eye. I managed to snap it closed before he poked my eyeball.

"He means the letter 'I,'" my father said. "See? He's spelling evil."

"Very good, Ryan," I said, ignoring my dad. "That's my eye." I set Ryan back on the floor. "Dad, do you think it's possible that Ryan is responsible for hiding your glasses?"

My father's laughter rumbled through the house. "What? You think your nephew is a mischief demon?"

"Stranger things have happened," I said. I watched Ryan as he returned to play with the figurines on the blanket on the floor. My stepmom never let Ryan play directly on the floor. There was always a blanket as a buffer between the toddler and her pristine carpet.

"I hope he's a more impressive mischief demon than you are a fury," my father said.

"Gee, thanks."

My dad came to stand beside me and gazed down at his grandson. "Do you really think he might be a mischief demon?"

"I don't know," I said. "But if you're not going senile or blind, then maybe there's another explanation."

"He looks like me, don't you think?" my dad asked with a proud smile.

Ryan gurgled and laughed as a trail of spit appeared on his chin.

I looked at my dad. "Yes, he definitely does."

My phone began to shriek like a banshee and I groaned.

"Did you change your mother's ringtone again?" my father asked.

"Variety is the spice of life," I replied, and clicked on the phone. "What is it, Mom?"

"Your nephew is missing! Call the hot chief of police."

I glared at my dad. I knew this would happen eventually. "Calm down, Mom."

"I can't calm down. My son is a vengeance demon. Do you know what he'll do to me if I let his son get dragged off from his crib by dingoes?"

"We don't have dingoes in this country," I said.

"They don't think we have witches and vampires in this country either, but we do."

I heaved a sigh. "Ryan is perfectly safe. I'm with him now."

"What do you mean?" The pitch of her voice pierced my ear and I winced.

"He wasn't sleeping so I decided to take him for a walk," I lied.

"Why didn't you leave a note?" my mom asked, her voice still shaking with outrage.

"A note? Uh, I guess I didn't think of it."

My mother clucked her tongue. "For a smart girl, you can be terribly dim-witted."

"I'll bring him back now."

"Please do. He needs his sleep. It's important for supernatural development."

I clicked off the phone and tucked it back in my pocket. "Let's go, Ryan. Back to your life behind bars."

Ryan held up his arms for me to lift him. "Up."

I picked him up and inhaled his powder scent.

"Why did you cover for me?" my father asked.

"Because I don't want the two of you fighting where I'll be caught in the middle." I smoothed Ryan's hair. "I covered for me, not for you."

"At least she said you were smart," he said. "That's a compliment."

"She said I was terribly dim-witted." And was probably plotting her revenge right now.

My dad shook his head. "Take the win."

"Please work out an arrangement if you want to see more of Ryan," I said. "Stealing him out of his crib isn't setting a great precedent."

"I'll think about it," my dad said stubbornly.

By the time I reached the backyard, I had to put Ryan on the ground to walk. He was far too awkward and heavy to carry on my hip the whole five hundred yards.

"They should make us carry toddlers at Quantico as part of our training," I told him. Not that it mattered now. All that training had been for nothing. I was here now, an agent for the FBM. And I'd have to endure basic supernatural training like some newbie. Life wasn't fair.

The walk took longer than necessary because Ryan kept falling every few feet, but we finally made it back to the farmhouse. My mother waited on the back step, her arms crossed.

"Take the scenic route, did you?" she asked.

"Mom-mom," Ryan said, and smiled.

My mother's frown faded. "Hello, you gorgeous little boy."

"You weren't this nice to me when I was little," I said. "You asked me to call you Beatrice in public."

"It seemed unnatural for you and Anton to call me anything else," my mom said. "I didn't look old enough to be anyone's mother."

"Is that why you've asked to be called Mom-mom?" I asked. "Because it could be mistaken for plain old mom?"

"Grandma was already taken," my mother sniffed. She lifted Ryan to her chest and tickled him under his chin. "Let's get you down for a nap, sweetheart." She turned and glanced at me over her shoulder. "I'll deal with you later."

Terrific.

I entered the kitchen where my grandmother and Aunt

Thora were slicing vegetables. Well, my great-aunt was slicing vegetables while my grandmother looked over her shoulder and criticized her. Teamwork.

"I know how to chop a carrot, Esther," Aunt Thora said.

Grandma looked at me. "I heard you kidnapped your nephew. If you want a baby so bad, why don't you go hang around the marina tonight? I'm sure someone can accommodate you."

"I didn't kidnap him." I refused to elaborate and rat out my dad, even though he deserved it.

"If you need a small sacrifice," Grandma said, "I'm sure we can poach a kid from the local school."

"I don't need a sacrifice," I said. "I don't practice black magic, remember?"

"You don't practice much of anything," Grandma said, snatching a carrot from the cutting board and biting into it. "If you did, you'd be better at your job."

I stiffened. "What makes you think I'm not good at my job?"

She waved the carrot at me. "Someone turned a vampire and you don't have a clue what happened."

I cocked an eyebrow. "How do you know about that?"

"The whole supernatural community is buzzing about it," Grandma said. "I heard about it from Nancy in the nursing home. I went to see her this morning."

My mother returned to the kitchen and gave me a sharp look. "Paul Pidcock would have had this situation under control by now."

"What situation?" I asked, exasperated. "We don't even know that there *is* a situation to get under control."

"Oh, there's a situation," my mother said. "I can feel it in the air. Can't you, Mom?"

"My spidey senses are tingling," Grandma agreed.

"That's just your overactive bladder," I said.

Grandma fixed me with a thousand yard stare. "You want to run my fade? Let's take it outside."

I closed my eyes, trying to collect myself. "I'm not going to fight you, Grandma, and for the love of Hecate, will you please stop reading the urban dictionary?"

"Wait until I tell Anton that you abducted his only son." Grandma dragged the end of the carrot across her neck in a threatening gesture.

I threw up my hands. "I'm going to my room." I was going to start carving a line in the wooden beam in the attic for every day I was still living here. I wished the carpenter had never bought that lottery ticket. Maybe the barn would be done by now.

"Run a brush through your hair while you're up there," my mother called. "You look like Ben Franklin had you tied to one of his kites during a storm."

I reached the top of the attic steps and slammed the door closed. I was so glad to be going out tonight. An evening with a misogynistic vampire had to be better than an evening with my family—didn't it?

CHAPTER SEVEN

EVERGREEN WAS a Georgian manor house dating back to the early 1800's. The house was set on fifty acres and included stables, an icehouse, and an orangery. The estate had been owned by the Robinsons, one of the few non-Puritan families that settled in Chipping Cheddar. The original owner, Walter Robinson, had been a mercantile ship's captain. The mansion had remained vacant throughout my childhood. Anton and I sometimes came here to practice our powers where there was little chance of being observed.

"Thanks for coming with me," I said to Clara. I parked the car on the long, tree-lined driveway.

"Rupert sounds like a loose cannon," Clara said. "No way would I let you come here alone and confront someone dangerous."

"*I'm* dangerous," I reminded her.

"But I know you," she said. "You'll avoid using your powers at all costs."

"True." I sighed. "Maybe you can touch his arm. Give me a reading on his emotions. If he's nervous, that might mean he knows something."

"Vampires are tricky because of the whole undead thing," she replied. "But I'll try."

"Thanks."

There were five other cars parked along the driveway, including a yellow Hummer. Whatever kind of club he was operating, it seemed to attract money.

As I reached for the doorbell, the door creaked open. Loud music pumping emanated from inside. Clara and I exchanged hesitant looks before entering the grand foyer. A scantily clad woman in heels immediately approached us with a tray of drinks.

"Welcome to Evergreen," the woman said. "Prosecco?"

"It might be poisoned," Clara whispered.

I plucked a flute from the tray and sniffed. "I don't sense anything magical. Just bubbles."

"Fine." Clara took a flute and drank. "You're right. Tastes normal."

"How much prosecco have you had in life to know what's normal?"

"It's one of Sassy's favorite drinks," Clara said.

I rolled my eyes. "Of course it is."

Clara's gaze sharpened. "You're making an effort with her, remember? I want you two to be friends."

"You're right. I'm sorry."

We took our drinks and followed the pulsating music to a ballroom at the back of the mansion. Five cars had somehow yielded more than twenty people. Unsurprisingly, all of the guests were female and under thirty. I didn't recognize anyone. The women eyed us closely as we entered and I suddenly felt like a new contestant on The Bachelor.

"Where's Rupert?" Clara asked.

"Maybe he likes to make an entrance."

Clara pointed to the pole in the middle of the room. "Maybe he'll slide down that like in a firehouse."

Inwardly, I groaned. "I don't think that pole is designed for transport."

I was about to mingle with one of the smaller groups when the music tempo changed and a handsome man entered the ballroom dressed in a traditional tuxedo. When he smiled, his fangs caught the light from the chandelier. Clara jerked beside me.

"It's not like you've never seen fangs before," I whispered.

"I know," Clara said. "I just wasn't expecting to see them on that guy. He looks like a prince."

I didn't disagree. With his wavy dark hair and penetrating dark eyes, Rupert could've easily passed for a European royal. His gaze alighted on us and he strutted over to greet us.

"I don't recall having the pleasure of meeting you two beauties before," he said. If eyes could devour, we would've been swallowed whole. The predator was strong in this one.

"I'm Eden," I said.

Clara offered her hand. "I'm Clara Riley."

"Enchanted." Rupert brought her hand to his lips and kissed it. I watched her eyelids flutter and she quickly pulled her hand away.

"I love that movie," Clara said. "I always sing when I clean, just like Giselle."

I pinched her side to snap her out of whatever stupor she was in. Clara winced and jerked away.

"If you'll pardon me," Rupert said, "the entertainment is about to begin."

The music changed again and the pulsating beat returned. One of the women screamed excitedly, as though anticipating something.

A moment later, I knew exactly what that something was. Rupert.

He began to dance around the pole, ripping off his bow tie as he moved.

"Are you seeing what I'm seeing?" Clara asked, fixated on the vampire.

"Unfortunately, I am. What did you feel when you touched him?"

"Lust," Clara replied. "It clouded every other emotion."

"Are you sure you weren't confusing your emotions with his?"

She glared at me. "The guy likes sex."

I observed his gyrating hips. "That's apparent."

"Wow. And here I thought he was a dignified vampire," Clara whispered.

"There's nothing dignified about what he's doing," I said, watching as Rupert wrapped his sinewy body around the pole. "I bet that's the attraction. He's probably spent an eternity as an uptight vampire with an immortality complex. He came to our town and boom!"

"Boom doesn't even begin to describe it."

We continued to watch in awe as Rupert stripped down to a G-string. "Looks like he's learned to embrace his manly parts."

"I think some of the women would like to embrace his manly parts," Clara said.

The women were whistling and cheering. I'd bet the elegant ballroom had never held any events like this prior to Rupert's tenure. If these walls could talk...

It occurred to me that these walls probably *could* talk. I tried to recall from my time spent here as a kid whether I'd ever encountered any ghosts. If one resided here, I might be able to learn more about Rupert, whether he'd turned anyone here.

"I'll be right back," I said to Clara. I turned around and walked smack into a familiar broad chest.

"We really have to stop running into each other like this," Chief Fox said. He rubbed his chest. "It hurts."

I swallowed hard. "What are you doing here?"

"I received an anonymous tip that the owner is operating an illegal strip club out of his house." He peered around me to see Rupert riding up and down the pole. "Seems my information was good."

"That's why I'm here," I said quickly. "Same intel."

"You sure about that?" he asked, suppressing a grin. "If memory serves, you've got a thing for strippers."

I wanted to dig a hole and bury myself under the floorboards. He was referring to our first meeting at The Cheese Wheel, where I'd drunkenly mistaken him for a stripper in his cop uniform.

"I don't have a thing for strippers," I insisted. "I like clothes. Lots of layers of them. I'm strictly here for the crime."

"You're cyber crime," the chief said. "Why would you be investigating this?"

"Online porn," I said quickly. "Someone's been posting his performances on the internet."

Chief Fox studied me for a moment. "We're not going to argue over jurisdiction, are we?"

"I'll make a deal with you," I said. "I'll leave you to it if you let me have two minutes with him first."

The chief's gaze flickered from the gyrating vampire and back to me. "If you think two minutes is all you'll need…"

I pressed my lips together. "I need to ask him a few questions. Then he's all yours."

"Fine."

No one noticed the chief of police in uniform—until he spoke. "I need everybody out. Show's over!" He clapped his hands, getting everyone's attention.

Rupert slid to the bottom of the pole and the music

screeched to a halt. "What's going on?" He approached us in his bright red G-string and I averted my gaze. Clara, on the other hand, couldn't look away if her life depended on it.

"I'm Chief Fox," he said. "Are you aware that this property isn't zoned for…whatever it is you're doing?"

"A zoning issue, Chief?" Rupert asked. "I need to apply for a variance to entertain women in my own home?"

The chief waved his hand. "You won't get a variance. You can't run a strip club out of your house."

"Well, that's disappointing," Rupert said. "I do so enjoy it."

"Apparently, one of your previous guests didn't enjoy it," Chief Fox said. "It seems someone stole her wallet while she was here. She thinks it was you."

"Me?" Rupert laughed. "I have more money than one could ever need and I'm imm…"

"Immature," I interjected. "He's very immature."

Chief Fox motioned to the cluster of guests. "Go home, people. Show's over. Make sure you all have your wallets."

"Are you going to arrest him?" I asked.

"I'm getting to that part," the chief said. "Don't rush me."

"I say the same thing," Rupert said. "I prefer to take my time and savor the moment." The vampire offered his wrists. "Go on. Handcuffs will complete the outfit."

"Two minutes, Chief," I reminded him.

Chief Fox hesitated before taking a few steps back. "I'm counting."

I pulled Rupert out of earshot of the chief. I couldn't risk being overheard. "Rupert, I need to make this fast. My name is Agent Eden Fury. I work for the FBM."

Rupert blinked. "You're law enforcement? I never would've guessed that."

"And I never would've pegged you for an amateur stripper, yet here we are." I angled him away from the chief. "I need to ask you a very serious question."

Rupert's lips curved into a sensual smile. "No, I don't have a girlfriend and yes, I'm very interested."

I ignored his comment. "Have you turned anyone since moving here?"

"Turned?" he repeated. "As in..." He snapped his fangs together.

"Yes, that."

"Why would I do that?" he asked.

"Because you can," I said. "Because you're the kind of vampire that runs a strip club out of his Georgian manor house."

"I have no interest in creating more vampires," he said. "I'm quite content with my own company." He smiled again. "Well, I do like attractive company, but only for the night." He nudged me. "Perhaps you'd like to come back once I've resolved this matter?"

"You swear you haven't stolen any money?" I asked.

"An outrageous accusation. I have plenty of my own."

"Why run a private strip club out of your home?"

"Why not if it makes others happy?" He eyed me closely. "I bet I can make you happy—several times, in fact."

I stiffened. "No, thank you."

Rupert leaned forward and inhaled my scent. "You reek of darkness. It's intoxicating."

"I think you've had a few too many proseccos," I said. "That's what's intoxicating." I steered him back to Chief Fox.

The chief's brow furrowed. "Did he just smell you?"

"He has an olfactory fetish," I lied.

Chief Fox handcuffed Rupert and guided him out of the mansion. Rupert twisted to look back at me, holding his hand to his ear like a phone. "Call me."

I waited until the mansion was empty before searching for any resident ghosts.

"Do I need to stay with you?" Clara asked. Her gaze flitted from room to room.

"What are you worried about? You're not going to see anything," I said.

"No, but I might feel their emotions if they're particularly strong." She shuddered. "Ghost feelings. Yuck."

"Fine, wait here."

Clara seemed to realize that she'd be left alone in the large foyer. "No, that's okay. I'll come."

I walked through the house, calling out to the spirits. Clara remained glued to my side, unwilling to separate from me. It wasn't until I reached the upstairs that I felt a presence.

"Hello?" I said. "Anyone here?" We stood in what appeared to be the master bedroom. The furniture was made from a rich mahogany and the decor was elegant yet modern.

An apparition appeared in the middle of the king-sized bed. "Boo."

"Boo?" I stared at the ghost of the older man with bushy white hair and matching facial hair. "That's your entrance?"

Clara gripped my arm. "There's a ghost?"

"No, I'm talking to the pillow," I said. "Of course there's a ghost." I inched toward the bed, dragging Clara with me. "I'm Eden."

The ghost observed me. "Greetings and salutations, Eden. My name is Samuel Robinson."

"This was your family's estate, I take it?"

"Once upon a time," the ghost said. "Now it belongs to that monster."

"Rupert?" I queried.

He floated above the bed. "My family would roll over in their graves if they knew what had become of our home. It's disgraceful."

"Why do you think he's a monster?" I asked. I wondered

whether Samuel had seen anything—maybe he'd seen Rupert turn Will into a vampire.

"Because he's a vampire," the ghost replied. "They're all monsters."

Ah. "Is he the first vampire you've encountered?"

"Of course not. What do you take me for?" He sailed over our heads and somersaulted around the room. His movements were making me queasy.

"You've known other vampires?" I asked.

"Chipping Cheddar has a portal that draws demons here," he snapped. "Don't you know anything?"

I gaped at him. His clothes suggested he'd been a ghost for over a century. "I'm just surprised that you were aware of such things…back then."

"I had the Sight," he said. "I could see them all. Vampires, werewolves, druids, demons." He sighed dreamily. "Mermaids. How I loved to watch them from the water's edge. There was a cove they liked to frequent. They thought it was private." He chuckled to himself.

"Mr. Robinson, have you ever seen Rupert do anything unusual?"

"What's unusual for a vampire?" he asked. "He likes to talk to himself in the mirror. Daily affirmations he calls them." The ghost made a dismissive sound. "Ridiculous I call them."

"He can see himself in a mirror?" I asked. Clara finally released my arm, and I rubbed the spot where she'd been digging in her fingers.

"He had someone charm the mirror," Samuel said. "I was here when he had it delivered. Came all the way from France."

"Did you ever see him hurt anyone?" I asked.

Samuel drifted over to the window. "Not in a painful way. He likes to fornicate, that's for sure. And the women seem to like to fornicate with him."

I held up a hand. "Okay, TMI."

"What's TMI?" he asked.

"Too Much Information," I said. "I don't need those kinds of details."

"You asked me if he ever hurt anyone," he said, clearly annoyed. "Sometimes, the women seemed to be in pain, but then they…"

"Thank you, Mr. Robinson," I said, cutting him off. Clara was lucky she didn't have to hear any of this. "You never saw him bite anyone? Draw blood?"

"Not in a nonconsensual sense," he said.

"Have you heard the name William Hickes spoken in this house?" I asked.

The ghost floated over to the mirror and pretended to admire himself, despite the absence of a reflection. "No, I can't say that name is familiar."

"You're certain?" I asked. "It's really important."

He looked thoughtful for a moment. "No. The only Hickes I knew were here more than a hundred years ago. They made cheese."

Who didn't, I wanted to say. "Thank you for your help, Mr. Robinson." Based on my conversation with Rupert and Samuel Robinson, I didn't think the vampire was connected to Will's situation.

"Do you think you might come back here again?" he asked.

"I don't think so," I said. I couldn't speak for Clara, though. She seemed to find Rupert far more appealing than I did.

"That's too bad," he said. "It gets lonely here in this big house."

"Can't you leave?" I asked.

"Leave?" Samuel appeared thoughtful. "I don't know. I've never tried."

"You've never tried to venture into town?" I asked. Talk about a limited imagination.

"It never occurred to me that I could," he said.

"Do you know why you're bound to this plane?" I asked.

His expression clouded over. "It's nothing I like to think about."

"I understand," I said. "Listen, there's a ghost at my house on Munster Close. Her name is Alice Wentworth."

The ghost lit up, as much as a wispy apparition could. "I remember the Wentworth farm. Alice, you say?"

"Yes, a very sweet woman. She lives in my house. Well, it was her house first, but you get the idea. Anyway, she ventures out every so often. Maybe the two of you could spend time together?"

"I would enjoy that very much," he said.

"Great, I'll speak to her about it. Thanks again for your help." I left the room and Clara hurried after me, not wanting to put any distance between us.

"Are you seriously playing matchmaker to ghosts?" she asked, once we were safely in the car.

"Why not?" I asked. "I bet Alice would appreciate the company. It can't be easy being a ghost."

Clara buckled her seatbelt. "You're something else, you know that?"

I started the engine. "Nothing new there. I've been something else my whole life." I turned the car around and, with a final glance in the rearview mirror, left Evergreen behind.

CHAPTER EIGHT

CLARA and I agreed to meet for coffee at The Daily Grind the next morning, mostly because she wanted to try the scone I was obsessed with. I'd just parked the car when a text came through from her.

Meet at Bugle instead. Behind schedule.

The Buttermilk Bugle office was only a block over from the coffee shop. I entered the small lobby and was nearly mowed down by Gasper Cawdrey. He looked exactly like his photo on the website.

"Is there breaking news somewhere?" I asked, only half joking.

"I parked in a handicapped spot and someone spotted Deputy Guthrie giving out parking tickets."

I stared at the gangly reporter. "You parked in a handicapped spot?"

"I hurt my knee playing rugby," he replied, as though that justified his actions.

I wasn't a fan of Sean Guthrie. The deputy and I attended high school together and shared a mutual dislike. That being said, I really hoped he got to Gasper's car before the reporter did. If I stalled him long enough, maybe I'd get my wish.

"You play rugby?" I asked. "That's a great sport. You must be pretty athletic." I did my best to feign interest.

"I work out a lot," Gasper said. He seemed to forget about his parking violation. "I like to keep fit. Don't want to develop my dad's beer gut."

"I don't blame you." I smiled and extended a hand. "I'm Eden Fury."

His brow shot up. "The new FBI agent?"

"That's right."

He shook my hand. "Gasper Cawdrey, the only source for news in Chipping Cheddar. If you ever need…"

The door flew open and Mitsy Malone strode into the lobby, clutching a rolled-up newspaper under her armpit. "Where's your boss?"

Gasper's mouth dropped open. "Miss Malone, how can we help you?"

She flipped her sunglasses to the top of her head. "Did I stutter? I need your boss."

"He's…He's not in right now," Gasper said. "But I can help you."

"My story was supposed to be on the front page," Mitsy said. She yanked the newspaper out from under arm and opened it. "Where is it?"

Gasper pointed to a photo of Mitsy on the page. "Right there, Miss Malone."

"That's the *bottom* page," Mitsy said, exasperated.

"No, it's still the front page," Gasper said. "It's just at the bottom."

"I'm below the fold," Mitsy cried. "This is unacceptable."

"I'm sure we can make it up to you," Gasper said.

Mitsy smacked the paper into his chest and he caught it. "See that you do." She spun on her heel and marched out.

"You interviewed her?" I asked.

"Yes, it was amazing," Gasper said. "She's the most famous person I've ever met."

"Do you know how she became famous?" I asked.

"Her YouTube channel," Gasper said. "It's about books."

"And this catapulted her to fame?"

"You'd have to watch it to understand."

I doubted it. There was something going on with Mitsy Malone and it had nothing to do with her YouTube channel.

"You should probably go move your car," I said. Deputy Guthrie had probably ticketed him by now.

"Right. My car." Gasper dashed out of the lobby with his alleged bad knee. What a jerk.

I continued into the office to find Clara. Her desk was right in the front. She was just applying a fresh coat of lipstick when I entered.

"Hey, I was about to leave," she said.

"Before we go, can I see the paper?" I asked. "The one with Mitsy Malone."

"Sure." Clara began to rummage around her desk.

Someone tapped me on the shoulder. "Here. Don't say I never gave you anything."

I turned to see Sassy Persimmons. "As long as it isn't herpes."

She whacked me in the arm with the newspaper. "Here's the article."

I scanned the front page, looking for clues to explain her mysterious rise to fame.

"You're a devoted fan, too?" Sassy asked. "I adore her. I was thinking of dying my hair red to look like hers."

"Me, too," I lied. "What do you know about her? I want to know *everything*."

Clara gave me a funny look but knew me well enough not to question it.

"Well," Sassy said, "we have so much in common. We both love chocolate ice cream and turtleneck sweaters." She gripped my arm excitedly. "Oh, and we both wished to be famous, like, every day since the day we were born." She swung her blond hair over her shoulder. "My time will come. I just know it."

"You should start a YouTube channel," I said. "About books."

"Oh, I could never compete with Mitsy," Sassy said. "Her channel is golden."

"Are you ready to go for coffee?" Clara asked.

Sassy glanced from Clara to me. "You're going for coffee without me?"

I gathered the courage to say a sentence I never thought I'd utter. "You're welcome to join us."

"Awesome, let me grab my purse." Sassy shot to her desk at the back of the office.

Clara offered a grateful smile. "What's with the interest in Mitsy?"

"There's something strange about her sudden fame," I said. "I'm trying to figure it out."

Clara lowered her voice. "You think magic might be involved?"

"It's possible. This is Chipping Cheddar, after all." I stopped talking when Sassy returned with her purse slung over her shoulder.

"Let's get caffeinated, ladies," Sassy declared. She turned and bounced out of the office ahead of us.

"I don't think she needs caffeine," I whispered.

Clara smiled. "You get used to her."

"I'll take your word for it." I tucked the newspaper into my handbag and followed my former nemesis out the door.

. . .

When I arrived home after coffee, the house was strangely quiet. I walked through the main rooms downstairs, but they were empty. Even the animals were out of sight.

"Hello?" I called, but no one answered.

I decided to try my mother's bedroom. I turned the knob and poked my head in.

"Mom?"

My mother was kneeling on the floor opposite Grandma. She immediately grabbed a nearby blanket and threw it across the floor.

My hands flew to my hips. "What's going on?"

"Nothing," my mother said quickly and rose to her feet.

"You look like I just caught you smoking pot," I said. "What are you up to?" The fact that Aunt Thora wasn't involved suggested nothing good.

Grandma deftly hopped to her feet in defiance of her eighty-odd years. "None of your business. You're an agent out there, not in here." She pointed to the floor.

"I'm an agent everywhere." I approached the blanket and yanked it off. I surveyed the ingredients on the floor—a frameless mirror, a few herbs, and candles. At least it didn't seem to be dark magic. "What spell are you conjuring?"

My mother folded her arms. "If you knew more about witchcraft, maybe you'd know without needing to ask."

"Seriously. Don't embarrass yourself, Eden," Grandma added.

"I'm going to figure this out." I took out my phone and snapped photos of the scene.

"Go ahead, Agent Fury," my mother smirked. "Give it your best investigative shot."

Ooh, now I was definitely going to get to the bottom of this. "You'd better hope it's nothing I'll disapprove of."

"Of course it's something you'll disapprove of," Grandma said. "Otherwise, we wouldn't bother hiding it from you."

My mother elbowed Grandma. "It's a spell to make sure that your brother's renovations pick up speed."

"Yeah, we're tired of sharing the house," Grandma said.

I eyed them both suspiciously. "Why don't I believe you?"

"Because you don't trust anybody," Grandma said. "That's one of your problems."

"One of my problems?" I echoed. "Of which I have many, apparently?"

"That's right. You think everyone falls short of your impossible standards," Grandma said.

"My standards are not impossible," I said. "You just don't like them."

"We're just being true to our nature, unlike *some* people," my mother said.

"I'm sorry I'm such a disappointment."

"You're young. There's still time to turn that around," Grandma said.

I groaned. "You'd better watch what you're doing. If I stumble upon something illegal, I won't have a choice but to report it."

"So you're a magic Nazi now?" Grandma asked. "We're allowed to do magic."

My mother was aghast. "You would turn in members of your own family? The woman who gave birth to you?"

"And the woman who gave birth to her?" Grandma pointed at my mother.

"I take my job seriously," I began.

"That's another one of your problems," Grandma interrupted. "You take everything seriously. You're as tight as Adele LeRoux's skin after a facelift spell."

"Why are you in my room anyway?" my mother asked. "This is my private oasis."

"I need a grimoire and I can't find the one I want," I said.

"Which one?" my mother asked. "I told you I use the internet."

"I want to look up spells that involve wishes," I replied.

My mother looked relieved. "Are you finally going to wish for clearer skin? I don't blame you, sweetheart. I'm surprised you put up with it for this long."

"There's nothing wrong with my skin," I said tersely. "I want to see what the spells involve."

My mother regarded me. "How badly do you want this?"

Uh oh. "Why?"

"I'll make a deal with you," she said.

"I am not going out with Hugh Phelps. He only wants to marry a werewolf," I said.

My mother smiled. "Forget about Hugh. Show me your wings and I'll get you the book."

I gasped. "You're blackmailing your only daughter?"

"It's not blackmail," Grandma said. "It's a deal. You both get what you want."

I hesitated. "No tricks? I show you my wings and you'll give me the grimoire?"

"I'll even let you keep it in the attic," my mother said. "Tuck it under your pillow and maybe you'll learn by osmosis."

"Fine." I took a deep breath and willed my wings to appear. Large black feathers unfurled from my back.

My mother's hand flew to cover her mouth. "They're gorgeous."

I peered over my shoulder to see them. "They're hideous."

"They match your hair," Grandma said. That was the closest thing to a compliment I'd get from her.

"Can I put them away now?" I asked.

My mother sighed contentedly. "If you must. I'll get the book." She went to her closet and reached for the top shelf, removing a large, leather-bound grimoire. "Here you go."

"Thank you." I took the book and began to flip through it. "They really should include an index in a book this thick."

"It was written before an index was a thing," my mother said. "But all the wish spells will be in the same section."

"Who wants tea?" Grandma asked.

"You're offering to make tea?" I asked.

"No, but Thora makes it every day around now," Grandma said. "I'm going to go put my order in."

Sure enough, we moved our party to the kitchen where Aunt Thora had just warmed the kettle. I sat at the table and continued to peruse the grimoire. I found the section I needed smack in the middle.

"There are a lot of different wish spells," I said.

Aunt Thora filled the teapot with water and put the teabags inside. "You want to do a wish spell, dear? Did that carpenter's winning the lottery inspire you?"

"No, it's this girl who's suddenly become famous." I stopped to look at her. "Winning the lottery is kind of a common wish, isn't it?"

"I would think so," my great-aunt replied.

"There's enough tea for me, right?" Grandma asked.

"There's always enough for you, Esther," Aunt Thora said.

I rested my hand on my chin. "What are the odds that more than one person had a wish spell cast at the same time?" It was unlikely enough that a human discovered magic. It was even more unlikely that multiple humans did within a five-mile radius.

"I bet it's that Rosalie LeRoux," Grandma said. "She likes to throw her magic around."

"She can't do that," I said. "These are humans with no knowledge of us."

"She acts like some kind of voodoo priestess who can get rid of curses," Grandma said. "She rents a place over on Asiago Street now."

"That's the same street as my office," I said.

"You're next to Holes, aren't you?" my mother asked. "Rosalie's place is three blocks south. You can't miss it. There's a tacky crystal ball in the window." She wrinkled her nose in disgust. "Brings down the whole neighborhood."

"Yes, it really dulls the shine of that tattoo parlor and the dollar store," I said. I glanced over the spells in the grimoire. "Do you really think she might be performing wish spells for people?"

"Rosalie would do anything for the right price," Grandma said. "I once saw her conjure a toupee for a guy in exchange for a taco."

Aunt Thora rolled her eyes. "Esther, that was *his* toupee that had blown into the street. Ernesto. He owns the taco truck by the promenade."

"Whatever," Grandma said. "All I'm saying is the witch likes her greenbacks. She's turned more tricks than a Vegas hooker."

I buried my face in my hands. "Nice analogy, Grandma." I closed the book and slid back my chair.

"No tea?" Aunt Thora asked.

"No, thanks," I said. "I'm going to see a voodoo priestess about a wish." I glanced at Grandma as I passed by. "And I might just request a custom curse while I'm there."

"Go ahead," Grandma said, raising her chin in defiance. "That'll bring you one step closer to our side. I know how appealing that is to you."

I grabbed my handbag and headed to Asiago Street. Instead of one step closer to Team Dark and Demented, I needed to be one step closer to figuring out the cause of these fortunate events—and, if I got my wish, Rosalie LeRoux just might have the answers.

CHAPTER NINE

ROSALIE'S PLACE was easy to spot thanks to the crystal ball in the window. Unlike my mother, I didn't find the display tacky. It was pure kitsch.

A little bell jingled when I opened the door.

"Twenty dollars," Rosalie said, not bothering to look up from her phone. Two tight braids peeked out from the bottom of her headscarf and she wore a purple kaftan. She looked like a younger version of Adele.

"Twenty dollars for what?" I asked.

She glanced up from the phone. "Eden Fury? For you, it'll be thirty."

I sat down across from her. "I think you swiped left twenty times since I walked in here. If you don't swipe right occasionally, you'll never meet anyone."

Rosalie set her phone facedown on the table. "I'm coming to the conclusion that meeting a man is a lost cause."

I snorted. "You should hang out with my mother. She's elevated it to an art form."

Rosalie leveled me with a look. "I think we both know that will never happen."

"I don't know," I said airily. "You both have a lot in common. No husbands. Over fifty. Overachieving daughters to moan about."

"Corinne *is* an accomplished witch," Rosalie said, a note of pride slipping into her voice. "So what brings you to see me? I seriously doubt this is a social call." Her eyes narrowed. "Your mother hasn't sent you here to hex me, has she?"

"Would I ever do my mother's bidding?"

Rosalie straightened. "I guess not. You always were more like a LeRoux than a Fury." She smiled. "Something that no doubt rankled your family to no end."

I ignored her remark. "Do you know who Mitsy Malone is?" I asked.

"Do I look like I've been living underground? Of course I do."

"Ever met her?"

Rosalie scrutinized me. "Why do you ask?"

"I was just wondering if she's ever been in here to see you."

Rosalie pinned her penetrating gaze on me. "You're here on FBM business, aren't you?"

She'd always been sharp—a LeRoux family trait. "I'm just asking a simple question about Mitsy Malone," I said.

"Why? You think I made her famous?" She threw her head back and cackled. "You think I'd waste my magic on something as frivolous as that?"

"Get real, Rosalie," I said. "I've seen you use magic to cut in line at the supermarket."

Rosalie blew a pouty breath. "If you really want to get into what's petty, we can talk about your precious grandmother's use of magic to cheat at bridge down at the senior center."

"Precious is not the word I'd use to describe Grandma," I

said. "But at least she doesn't con unsuspecting humans out of money."

"I'm not conning anybody, sugar. It's a simple case of supply and demand. Those who desire my services know where to find me. I'm word-of-mouth only."

"How can you run a business like this with your mother on the supernatural council?" I asked.

Rosalie lifted a finely sculpted eyebrow. "There's not a total ban on magic in this town, Eden Fury. I don't flaunt it and I don't cause anyone harm."

"Magic always comes at a price," I said.

Rosalie smiled. "Yes, and that price is twenty dollars. Thirty if you need a curse removed." Her smile faded. "Or if your name is Fury."

"But you're conning people into believing they carry a curse in the first place."

"No, I'm not." She wore an indignant expression. "Just last week, a young man came in here with a limp."

"So?"

"It wasn't a medical issue," she said. "Someone had hexed him."

"How can you be so sure?"

"Because by the time he walked out of here, the limp was gone. You know I wouldn't be able to do that if the limp hadn't been magic-induced."

She was right. "And he knew to come in here to get rid of his limp?"

"He's friends with one of the Phelps boys," Rosalie said. "They made a gentle suggestion to see me. Told him I was a practitioner in the healing arts."

"Any idea who hexed him?" I asked. Maybe it was someone I needed to keep tabs on.

Rosalie's mouth quirked. "Who do you think?"

I exhaled. "Which one—Grandma or Mom?"

"From the story he told me, sounds like your grandma," Rosalie said. "Apparently, he took her parking spot downtown. By the time he left his car, he had two flat tires and a limp."

Oh boy. "And he knows my grandmother is responsible?"

"Of course not. I hypnotized him first to get the story."

Small mercies. "So, in a way, my family sends you business." This fact did not make me feel better.

"Sugar, your family paid for the addition on our house two years ago." She flipped her phone back over and began to peruse her dating options again. She swiped left.

"What was wrong with him?" I asked. "He seemed okay."

She held the phone closer to her chest. "He doesn't drink. I don't trust a man who abstains from alcohol." She paused. "I don't trust a man who abstains from anything."

"You should meet Rupert."

"The new vampire in town?" She flicked a finger. "Too young for me."

"The immortal vampire is too young for you?"

"He'd never be faithful," Rosalie said. "I'm looking for a commitment."

"Fair enough."

"Any other questions, Agent Fury, or do you just want to critique my dating preferences?"

"Do you know anything about John, the carpenter who won the lottery?" I asked.

Rosalie frowned. "Yes, I heard about him. Nice fella, by the sound of it."

"I take it he didn't come in here either?"

"No." She set her phone back on the table, suddenly interested in the conversation. "I see what you're getting at. You think someone's granting wishes."

"I do."

"And you immediately thought of me."

"Can you blame me?"

Rosalie smirked. "I am considered gifted in that particular area."

"But it wasn't you."

She shook her head. "Sorry, sugar. Fame and lottery winnings? That's too much magic. I'd never risk it."

"Can you think of anyone who would?"

"Outside of your family, not really."

I slumped in the chair. "I really hoped it was you."

Rosalie was silent for a moment. "Have you considered a wish demon?"

A light bulb switched on in my head. "Sweet Hecate. That makes so much sense."

She harrumphed. "Maybe I should have taken over Paul Pidcock's job."

"Cut me some slack," I said. "This is all new to me. I don't have experience tracking supernatural suspects."

"So glad the FBM decided to put you in charge here. I feel so safe."

I glared at her. "It's going fine so far."

"Three people died already."

"Technically two. Paul Pidcock died before I got here and I caught the fear demon responsible."

"See? We've already had a fear demon. Is it such a stretch to consider a wish demon?"

"No, it's actually a good suggestion." I was annoyed that I didn't think of it myself.

I'd never even encountered a wish demon. By all accounts, they were unusual in this world. Not as rare as a fury, but rare enough.

"I don't suppose you have any wish demons in your family," Rosalie said.

"Unfortunately not."

"Didn't think so. They tend to be benevolent. Wouldn't fit your family tree."

I bit the inside of my cheek to keep from hexing her. I may not be a fan of my family's gene pool, but I had a twisted sense of loyalty toward them. Like most families, our relationships were complicated.

"Must be tough for you," she continued, "living with your family again when you were so desperate to get away."

"I'm moving into the barn," I said. "As soon as it's renovated."

"Well, it's not three thousand miles, but I guess it's better than nothing."

"Thanks for the help, Rosalie." I tossed thirty dollars onto the table. "Can I get a receipt?"

"A receipt?"

"Yes. This counts as a business expense."

"Look at you, so official." She scribbled the amount on a piece of paper and signed it. "Good luck to you, sugar."

I left Rosalie and began to walk the few blocks to my office, deep in thought. If a wish demon was to blame, then I had to stop it from granting any more wishes and send it back to Otherworld. If I could determine where the wishes had been made, that might lead me to the demon.

I pulled out my phone and checked Mitsy's social media accounts to see if I could track her down. A photo of her posing in Rockefeller Center told me I was out of luck, at least for a few days.

Thankfully, I still had one more option.

I bypassed my office and headed toward the marina. It was time to see how John's Great American Novel was coming along.

John's new boat wasn't hard to locate. I figured everyone in town would know where the lottery winner kept his boat and I wasn't wrong. I only had to ask the first person I saw.

"Hey, John," I called from the dock.

He peered at me from the deck. "Barn girl?"

That was the way he remembered me? Okay then. "Eden," I said.

"That's right." He tipped back his baseball hat. "Are you here to see me?"

"I am, actually."

He beckoned me forward. "Welcome aboard, Eden. Happy to have you."

His skin looked a shade darker than when I'd met him in the barn.

"Nice boat," I said.

"Thanks, it's a dream come true," he said. He walked to a cooler and pulled out a beer bottle. "Care for one?"

"No, thanks."

He popped off the lid and took a long swig. "This is the life."

"What do you do all day?" I asked.

"Fishing, water ski. You name it."

"I heard you were writing a book," I said.

"I work on my novel in the evenings," he said. "I don't like to miss the sun."

"I can see that." I gestured to his tanned skin.

He examined his arms. "Should probably apply a little more sunscreen. I'm used to working inside structures all day." He leaned a hip against the side of the boat. "What brings you here?"

"I was hoping you could recommend another guy for the barn job," I said. "I'm eager to get it done so I can move in."

He chuckled. "Eager to get out of the family nest, huh? I can understand that, having met..." He stopped abruptly. "Well, we all want distance from our families, don't we?"

So much for my mother's plan to date him. "Anyone come to mind for the job?"

He took another drink. "Sure. I've got a few names. Want me to write them down for you?"

"I can just put them in my phone," I said.

"Lawrence Masterson does a good job," John said. "He lacks vision, but he's proficient."

"Do you miss it yet?" I asked.

He hesitated. "I'd be a fool to miss it, right? I mean, I'm living the dream."

"That certainly seems to be the case." It wouldn't be *my* dream, but to each his own.

John's facade cracked. "Who am I kidding? This whole thing sucks." He whipped off his hat and tossed it aside. "I'm bored out of my mind. I can't write a book. I don't even like to read that much."

"Then why all this?" I spread my arms wide.

"It's what I thought I always wanted. The thing I wished for with every penny in the fountain, you know?" He gazed across the water. "I never expected my wish to come true."

"Who does?" I said. "Have you considered not quitting your job? There's no requirement that you quit when you win the lottery. We'd still love for you to work on the barn."

"But where's my incentive to finish the job and move on to the next one if I don't need the money?" he asked. "I'll drag my heels. You'll get impatient and fire me."

"Then don't drag your heels," I said.

"I think I'm someone who needs structure in my day. All this free time…it's not good for me."

I could empathize with him because I was the same. I thrived in a structured setting. Too much freedom would unravel me.

"What about living on the boat?" I asked. "That must be a plus."

He shrugged. "I kind of miss my neighbors. We have this neighborhood fire pit that's really cool. We all hang out there on the weekends."

"No one visits you here?"

"A few people have come by, but it's not the same."

"Why don't you just keep the boat for fishing and other activities and move back into your place?"

He stroked his chin. "I guess I could. I haven't sold it yet."

"And I imagine you haven't spent all your money yet."

"No, the boat was obviously my big purchase," he said. "I'm planning to invest the rest."

At least he was prudent. "Just out of curiosity, where did you buy your lottery ticket?" Maybe the wish demon had been the one to sell him his ticket, although that wouldn't explain Mitsy.

"Same place I always buy my ticket," he said. "The convenience store downtown. Abilene always waits on me." He smiled. "I think she was as thrilled as I was when I won."

"Abilene Forrester?"

"That's her."

Abilene wasn't a wish demon. She'd worked at the convenience store since I was a kid. I would have recognized her true nature years ago.

"Why do you ask?" John said. "You think lightning might strike twice?"

I smiled. "My grandmother insists she's feeling lucky, so I told her I'd buy her one at the same place you won." The lie slid off my tongue with ease.

"Others have had the same thought. I stopped in for milk the other day and Abilene said they've been swamped with people buying lottery tickets."

My phone vibrated in my pocket. I pulled it out to see Anton's name. "Would you excuse me for a second?" I turned my back to answer. "What is it, Anton? I'm kind of in the middle of something."

"I need your help. Could you please pick up Olivia from school? Verity and I are stuck at work."

"What about Mom or Dad?" I asked.

Anton paused. "They've both been banned from school grounds."

"By Verity?"

"No, by the school." He sighed. "It's a long story that involves an argument in the parking lot when they both showed up to collect her at the same time."

"Does it involve magic?" I whispered.

"Not as far as the school knows," Anton said.

Good grief. "I'll be there as fast as I can."

"Thanks, Eden. You're the best."

I tucked away the phone and spun around to face John. I'd have to continue my questions another time. "I'm sorry, but I need to go pick up my niece from school. It's been great talking to you, though. If you decide to work on the barn, let me know as soon as you can."

"Before you go…" His grip on the beer bottle tightened. "Do you think you might be interested in going out with me sometime?"

I blinked. "On a date?"

"Sure. Why not? Unless you have a thing against lottery winners."

"I don't know, John," I said. "You might be working on my future home. You don't think that might be awkward?"

"One date," he said. "No big deal if we decide we don't like each other. We're both grownups."

I hesitated, quickly running through the pros and cons in my mind. A date *would* give me more time to question him and that was the priority.

"Okay. What do you have in mind?"

He smiled, his relief evident. "How about Chophouse tonight?"

"Maybe somewhere else?" I asked. Dinner at Rafael's restaurant guaranteed that my mother would find out.

He scratched the back of his neck. "You don't like the most popular restaurant in town?"

"I do, but it's always so busy and loud," I said. "Makes it hard to have a real conversation."

John's eyes crinkled at the corners. "Quiet conversation sounds good to me. How about you give me your number and I'll text you the plan?"

"Sure." I gave him my number. "I'll see you tonight."

"Great. I'm looking forward to it."

I raced back to the car, not wanting to keep my niece waiting. I felt a little guilty for agreeing to go out with John just to question him about his wish, but I wasn't willing to turn down the opportunity to get more information. There was too much at stake. At least we'd both get a decent meal out it, which—according to Clara—was the definition of a good date.

CHAPTER TEN

I MET John at the restaurant so that no one in my family knew about it, at least not immediately. I used my invisibility locket to get out of the house unseen. One look at my outfit and my mom would know I was going on a date. Lipstick alone would've been a dead giveaway because I rarely wore makeup, much to her chagrin. She'd even spelled my eyes in middle school with longer lashes because she felt mine were "substandard" and lacked "batting ability."

"You look pretty," John said, giving me the once-over.

John had left his baseball hat behind. Tonight he wore a light blue collared shirt that showed off his tan and neatly pressed khakis.

"Thanks, you look nice, too. I like the sandals."

He glanced down at his feet. "I couldn't bring myself to put on real shoes," he said. "That's one of the perks about living and working on the boat."

The hostess seated us at a table by the window, which was fine by me because I liked to people watch. I figured if the conversation was dull, then I still had an activity to occupy my mind without being super obvious about it.

"What looks good to you?" John asked, inclining his head toward the menu.

"I basically will eat any type of seafood," I said.

"Same. Want to share the grilled shrimp appetizer?"

"Sounds delicious." I ended up ordering crab cakes for my entree. I couldn't resist Maryland crab, even though it was on pretty much every menu in town.

I ordered a glass of white wine and John ordered a beer. Although the conversation started out stilted, we both seemed to relax after our first drink. I decided it was the ideal time to dig a little deeper into his lottery win.

"So have you always played the lottery?" I asked.

"Every week for—oh, I don't know—a number of years now. Just was a habit when I'd stop in for my milk and bread, you know?"

"But you seem to enjoy your work," I said. "What made you think money would improve your life?"

"Doesn't everybody think money would improve their life?" he asked. "I mean, I feel like winning the lottery is on most people's wish list."

"I've never actually played," I admitted.

John's eyed widened. "Really? I don't think I've ever met anyone who hadn't played on occasion."

"I guess I've been motivated by things other than money." Which was easy to say when I've always had enough of it.

"I'd be hammering away and daydreaming about what I would do with a million bucks." He popped a shrimp into his mouth. "Passed the time."

"And now that you have it, you're not too enamored?"

He hung his head. "Life's funny that way, isn't it?"

"At least you're smart enough to figure it out," I said. "That's more than I can say for a lot of people."

"You're right about me, by the way," he said. "I do love my job, or I did, before I was stupid and packed it in. I kept my own hours and fished when I felt like it. And it's not like I need a lot of money to be happy here. My needs are pretty simple."

The appetizer quickly disappeared and the waitress returned with our main dishes. It smelled wonderful and I couldn't wait to dig in. As I sliced my fork through the first crab cake, I glimpsed Chief Fox outside on the sidewalk. He stood in front of the window, in the midst of a conversation with someone out of view.

No, no. Not here. Don't come in, I willed.

He came in.

Chief Fox was accompanied by a petite blond woman. She had her arm linked through his and was smiling up at him adoringly.

My stomach lurched.

Okay, that was ridiculous. Why did I care if the chief ate dinner with a pretty blonde? We weren't involved. We *couldn't* be involved. And the chief seemed like a reasonable guy. If he liked her, then she was probably perfectly acceptable.

He noticed me and waved. I wanted to blend into the wallpaper or close my locket and disappear, but instead I sat there and smiled.

"Good evening, Agent Fury," the chief said, approaching our table. His gaze flicked to John. "And who's your friend?" I noticed the question came out a little stiff.

"John," he replied. He stood and shook the chief's hand.

"John, this is Sawyer Fox, the new chief of police," I said.

John offered a friendly smile. "Right. I've heard about you. Nice to put a face to the name."

"How do you two know each other?" the chief asked.

"We met in my barn," I said. Ugh, not the best answer I could've given, but I was still reeling from the chief's presence. His hair was slightly damp from what I assumed was the shower and he wore a body-skimming black T-shirt with tight gray pants. Did he have to look as good in street clothes as in his uniform? It seemed grossly unfair to the rest of the men in the world.

The chief gave a halfhearted laugh. "The barn, huh? Okay, that doesn't sound odd at all." He shifted toward his companions. "This is my friend from out of town, Audra."

Audra plastered on a smile, but it looked more like she'd sucked one of Aunt Thora's lemons. "Pleased to meet you both."

"Are you from Iowa?" I asked. I knew the chief was originally from Des Moines.

"We went to the University of Iowa together," Audra said. "I live in Chicago now."

"You picked a good time to visit here," John said. "Weather's been perfect."

"Yes, Sawyer's been talking it up so much, I just had to come and see for myself."

"Chipping Cheddar is a special place," John said.

"I'm still on the fence," Audra said. "Only one good coffee place? Even the crappy town I grew up in had two good coffee places."

I had to fight the urge to hex her with a silencing spell. Yes, yes. I was a hypocrite. Even though I'd avoided living here and had to be dragged back kicking and screaming, I'd still defend my hometown to anyone who tried to put it down.

The chief nudged Audra. "Come on. You can't base your entire opinion of a town on its coffee offerings. You said earlier that the downtown was great."

Audra stroked his arm. "I was being polite."

"Chief Fox, your table is ready," the hostess said.

Thank the gods.

"It was good to meet you, John. Enjoy your dinner." The

chief's gaze lingered on me for a moment longer before he turned and followed the hostess to another table across the room.

"He seems nice," John said. "A fair bit younger than Chief O'Neill."

"Definitely."

"Didn't seem like his girlfriend was very impressed with our neck of the woods."

"You think Audra is his girlfriend?" I craned my neck for another glimpse of them.

John shrugged. "She was hanging on him like she was. Might as well have peed in a circle around him to keep the other females at bay."

I laughed. "I think it's only male animals that do that."

"Well, she lives in Chicago. Maybe they do things differently there."

I cracked another smile. John was turning out to be good company, even if I wasn't particularly attracted to him.

"Have you dated a lot here?" I asked.

"Not as often as I'd like," John said. "I tend to get caught up in a project and then not make time for much else besides fishing."

"My brother likes to fish in the river not far from the mound," I said.

"That's where my buddy Joe likes to go," John said. "We were just there a couple weeks ago, talking about winning the lottery, in fact. What are the odds, right?"

Hmm. Could a wish demon be in the river? "You were fishing at the time?"

"I guess. We'd gone for a hike and then headed to the river to relax."

"And Joe said his wish was to win the lottery, too?"

John chuckled. "No, actually Joe said he'd wish I'd win the lottery so I'd stop talking about winning the lottery."

"My brother always says the best catches are in the river." I neglected to mention that Anton also thought the dormant portal in the mound was somehow a draw for the fish. Why, I had no idea. It wasn't like the fish were supernatural.

"He's right. I always get lucky there." John's face turned beet red. "With fishing, I mean."

"With the lottery, too, apparently," I said. "That's where you talked about winning and then, lo and behold, you did."

John polished off his second beer. "Yeah, I guess you're right. Maybe I should take my next date there."

We laughed, though I thought it was interesting that he made no mention of taking me there. He was either a total gentleman or had already decided he wasn't interested.

"If you'll excuse me, I need the restroom," I said. I wanted to text Neville about researching wish demons that lived in rivers.

"Take your time. I promise not to eat your food," he said.

I hurried to the restroom and shot off a quick text to Neville before disappearing into a stall. When I emerged, I saw Audra at the sink, reapplying lipstick while she admired her reflection in the mirror. She noticed me and popped the lid back on the tube of lipstick.

"Sawyer sure has a lot to say about you," she said. She talked to me via her reflection, which was weird.

I washed my hands quickly, eager to return to the table and away from Audra. "Well, we worked on a case together recently."

"He said you're some kind of cyber crime fighter. Sounds pretty lame to sit in front of a computer all day."

"And what do you do, Audra?"

"I'm a physician's assistant at a big hospital," she said. "One of the biggest in Chicago."

"Is that like a nurse?"

Her eyes hardened like two dark stones. "No, it is *not* like a nurse."

I frowned. "Is there something wrong with being a nurse?"

"How do you not know what a physician's assistant is?" she asked. She was still talking to me in the mirror, even though I was looking directly at her.

"I guess I've never encountered one," I said. "My sister-in-law is a doctor, but she has her own practice." And I'd been fortunate enough not to spend time in any hospitals.

Audra glared at me. "I think you're just trying to insult me because of Sawyer."

Now I was very confused. "Insult you? Nurses are amazing. How is that an insult?"

"You know how."

Audra was making me dizzy. "Why would I want to hurt your feelings if you're a friend of the chief's? I like the chief." More than I cared to admit.

Audra slipped the lipstick into her handbag. "Because we're more than friends. He and I have been involved off and on since college."

"That's nice." I dried my hands as she continued to stare at me in the mirror.

"I don't like to hear him talk about other women," Audra said.

"I guess that's an issue you'll need to raise with him then." I smiled sweetly. "How long are you in town?"

"Hopefully not much longer," she said. "It's great to see Sawyer, of course, but I'm bored out of my mind. I can't wait to get back to Chicago."

I couldn't imagine being bored in the chief's presence.

"Sawyer is amazing, but I could never marry him unless he moved to Chicago," she continued. "He loves insignificant places like this and I left them far behind when I left Iowa. I have no desire to go back to that life."

My heart stuttered. "Has he asked you to marry him?" The question slipped out before I could stop myself. I'd been trying to play it cool, but curiosity got the better of me.

"No, but he would if I wanted him to," she said. "I'm the kind of woman who gets what I want. You'd do well to remember that, Agent Furry."

"It's *Fury*," I said.

"Whatever." Audra sailed out of the restroom without a backward glance. I watched her go, pleased to see that she left with a piece of toilet paper stuck to the bottom of her shoe.

I returned to the table feeling a little off-kilter. I wondered what the chief had actually said to make Audra think I was a threat to their relationship. The chief had said before that he wasn't married because he was married to the job. There'd been no mention of Audra, or any other girl-friends. So how did Audra fit in?

"You okay?" John asked.

I flashed a bright smile. "Yes, good. The food is delicious."

"Is it? Because you've barely eaten any."

I glanced down at my full plate. "I like to save half for the next day. Savor the experience."

John eyed me closely. "You're not into this, are you?" He motioned between us.

"I'm having a nice time," I said.

"But there's no spark," he said.

I shifted uncomfortably in my seat. "I don't think so, do you?"

Relief washed across his features. "No."

We both laughed and I instantly relaxed.

"I hope you're not too disappointed," I said.

"Hey, as long as we're on the same page, it's all good," John said. "And the bonus is that I still get to renovate your barn." He paused. "Right?"

"Are you sure?"

"I am." He scraped the last of his food off his plate. "So how long have you had a crush on the new chief? He is pretty good-looking for a dude."

The back of my neck warmed. "I don't have a crush on the chief."

"You don't have to pretend with me," John said. "I could feel the energy between you two. Pretty sure that old guy across the room felt it, too, and he's asleep."

"There's no energy," I insisted.

John suppressed a smile. "Whatever you say, Eden."

We split the bill when it came and John walked me back to my car. I noticed the chief glance in my direction as we left, but I didn't acknowledge him.

"This was fun," John said. "Let's do it again sometime. As friends, of course."

"On one condition," I said.

"What's that?"

"That you never date my mother," I said.

John hunched over, his shoulders shaking with laughter. "In all my years of dating, I've never had that specific request."

"Seriously, if you do the barn, she's bound to hit on you. Please put her off as nicely as possible. Tell her you're engaged. Or you're moving to Guam. Whatever it takes." My mother wasn't one to take no for an answer. John would have to be firm but kind, or else she'd hex him, not that I could tell him that.

John didn't even hesitate. "Deal," he said.

CHAPTER ELEVEN

WHEN I GOT HOME, I tried to sneak past the kitchen and head straight to the attic to change into cozy pajamas. I didn't think about using the locket until it was too late.

"There's Eden now," I heard my mother say.

I froze mid-step.

"Eden, come see who's here," Grandma called.

Reluctantly, I turned and entered the kitchen. My grandmother's best friend, Shirley, sat at the table with Mom, Grandma, and Uncle Moyer. Candy was sprawled across the table, her tail flicking the cards across the surface.

"Gin rummy?" I asked.

"What else?" Shirley asked. "Come closer so I can get a good look at you. It's been too many years."

Shirley was a tall, busty woman with cropped white hair and a penchant for chunky jewelry. She was a human with the Sight and a psychic, though I often doubted her abilities. Her predictions tended to be on par with those found in Chinese fortune cookies or horoscopes.

"You look just the same," I said.

"Lying is a sin, Eden Fury," she chastised me.

"So is gambling," I said.

Shirley gestured to the cards. "This is gin rummy. Perfectly acceptable. Now poker is another matter entirely."

"Which is why we can't play and I'm stuck being the dealer," Uncle Moyer interjected, sounding vaguely put out.

I greeted him with a kiss on the cheek. "Where's Tomas?" Tomas was Uncle Moyer's husband and a human-angel hybrid.

"He has a cold," Uncle Moyer said. "You know what a baby he is when he has the sniffles. You'd think he was on death's door."

"Throw salt over your shoulder when you say a thing like that," Shirley told him. She was as superstitious as she was pious.

Uncle Moyer took a pinch of salt from the shaker and threw it over his left shoulder, his expression deadpan.

"Now tell me, Beatrice," Shirley said. "Why hasn't there been a party to welcome Eden home? I would think it's a cause for celebration."

"I would have planned one, but *someone* didn't tell us she'd be moving back until the last minute." My mother maintained a neutral expression, as though the identity of that someone was a complete mystery.

"The transfer was unexpected," I said. "Besides, you know I wouldn't want a party." Being the center of attention in this house never ended well and was best avoided.

"So, Eden, how was your date?" my mother asked.

I flinched. "How did you know I was on a date?"

Grandma jerked her hand of cards in Shirley's direction. "We're entertaining a psychic. How do you think?"

"You had a vision of me on a date?" I asked.

Shirley set down a run of diamonds. "No, Mona saw you out with that lottery-winning carpenter and texted me."

I felt my mother's laser eyes burning a hole through me. I ignored her and went to put my leftovers in the fridge.

"Bring over a snack for the table while you're up," Grandma said.

I rummaged in the pantry, careful to avoid anything that looked earmarked for a spell. I'd made that mistake in high school and ended up with a swollen nose for a week. I'd had to invent a story about walking into a sliding glass door.

I pulled a bag of mixed nuts from the shelf and brought them to the table to pour into a bowl.

Grandma cringed. "I said a snack, not brains."

"These are nuts."

"You're nuts," Grandma said. "You know I'm allergic. Are you trying to kill me?"

"Mom, you're not allergic," my mother said. "You just don't like walnuts."

Grandma pushed the bowl away. "That's an understatement. You're basically eating brains."

Uncle Moyer crooked a finger, gesturing for the bowl. "Consider me a zombie then because I adore walnuts."

"Maybe that's how you got so smart, Moyer," Shirley said. "Eating all those tiny brains."

"He certainly didn't inherit it from his mother," Grandma said.

"Grandma! That's a horrible thing to say about your sister," I told her. I glanced around the room. "Where is Aunt Thora?"

"She retired early," my mother said. "My grandchildren were full of beans this evening and wore her out."

I guess that explained why Anton and Verity were nowhere to be seen as well.

"Would you like to play, Eden?" Shirley asked. "I could use a little competition. The rest of the players aren't really up to my standards."

"You think God isn't up to your standards," Grandma shot back.

"And what about the young carpenter?" my mother asked. "Does he meet your exacting standards, Eden?"

I knew we'd circle back to my date at some point. It was only a matter of time.

"Your mother tells us he's quite handsome," Moyer said.

"John is attractive," I said. "I can't argue with that."

"Oh," my mother sniffed. "So it's *John* now, is it?"

"They had dinner together," Grandma said. "What do you think she should call him? Guy My Mother Wants To Bone? He's not Native American."

"We ended the date as friends," I said. "And he wants to renovate the barn."

My mother perked up. "He does? But what about his boat and writing the Great American Novel?"

"It's not the life for him, apparently," I said. "He wants to continue to do carpentry."

"What a waste of a winning lottery ticket," Grandma said.

Shirley fanned out her cards in front of her face. "Playing the lottery is a sin anyway. It's no wonder he found no peace from his winnings. That kind of money is Satan's work."

Moyer arched an eyebrow. "You remember you're sitting at the table with a demon, right?"

Shirley smiled and swatted his arm. "Oh, Moyer. You know I don't mean you."

"So you're only racist about demons you don't know?" I suggested.

"Shirley's known plenty of demons she hasn't liked," Grandma said. "Remember Patty Sinclair?"

Shirley groaned. "Do I ever? I had to beg forgiveness on that one. Went to church every day for a month in penance." Shirley raised her eyes to the heavens.

"What did you do?" I asked.

Shirley and Grandma exchanged looks. "I gave her a reading," Shirley said.

"She lied and told Patty that her husband was cheating on her," Grandma interrupted, and laughed. "You should've seen Patty's face. I hadn't seen a face as pale as that since your father brought Sally home from Otherworld."

"What happened to Patty's husband?" I asked.

"Apparently, he confessed and they went to marriage counseling," Shirley said.

Grandma cackled. "We couldn't believe it. Turns out he had a thing with their babysitter. Nobody had a clue."

"Still, I shouldn't have committed a sin like that simply because I disliked the woman," Shirley said. "It was petty and unnecessary."

"Do unto others," Uncle Moyer said, nodding sagely.

"Why, Moyer. That's from the Bible," Shirley said. "Isn't there some rule about demons quoting the Bible? Doesn't your tongue burn?"

Uncle Moyer flashed a devilish grin. "He who lacks knowledge, lacks quotable material."

Shirley straightened in her chair. "Anyhow, the way I see it, I actually ended up saving their marriage. They should have thanked me."

"Yes, you're doing God's work," Grandma said. Shirley seemed oblivious to the sarcasm, or chose to ignore it. After all these years, I had no doubt she was accustomed to my grandmother's sharp tongue.

"Well, I'm glad John has committed to working on the barn," my mother said. "That's one less item on my list."

"You're just happy because you'll get to watch him work," Grandma said.

"Please don't stalk him," I said. "I want him to finish the barn so I can move in."

"Let your mother stalk him," Grandma said. "Then he'll be inclined to work faster so he can get out of here."

My mother began to pout. "I'm a catch, I'll have you know."

Uncle Moyer patted her hand. "Of course you are, Beatrice."

"Speaking of a catch, does anyone know of a wish demon that's partial to rivers?" I asked.

"A wish demon?" Grandma queried. "Do we have one of those in town now?"

"I thought it was a wish spell you were after," my mother said.

"I don't think it's a spell anymore," I said. "Rosalie LeRoux suggested…"

My grandmother made a noise at the back of her throat. "You're going to listen to that charlatan?"

"You're the one who sent me to see her," I said.

"I was hoping you'd just arrest her and send her to Other-world," Grandma said. "No questions asked."

I crossed my arms over my chest. "That's not how it works."

"Why not?" Grandma asked. "I certainly won't tell."

I pursed my lips. "Anyway, Rosalie suggested a wish demon and I think she might be right."

"Why a river?" Shirley asked.

"John said he was fishing at the river when he wished to win the lottery," I said. "I need to find this demon before anyone else gets their wish."

"You're like the anti-Santa Clause," Shirley said.

"I think that's the Grinch," Grandma replied.

"Seriously, Eden," my mother said. "Why do you have to put a damper on everyone's fun?"

"You know why," I replied.

"Eden's right," Uncle Moyer said. "It's important to preserve the balance."

"It's important to preserve blackberries," Grandma shot back. "Granting wishes isn't evil. It makes people happy. I would think you'd be all in favor of that, Miss Goody Two Shoes."

"Too much magic upsets the natural order, whether good or bad," I said.

"Oh, come on," my mother said. "Let the people have their fun. I'm sure the wish demon will slink off into the sunset eventually. No harm done."

There was no point in arguing with my family. We'd never agree on the subject.

"It could be worse," Shirley said. "John could've been turned into a vampire like that poor Hickes boy. If that doesn't upset the natural order, then I don't know what does."

"You know about Will?" I asked. Did the gossip ever take a rest in this town?

"It's not necessarily worse," Uncle Moyer said. "I've had plenty of clients offer their souls in exchange for immortality."

"What did you say?" I turned to stare at my uncle.

"Now, Eden, you don't need to take issue with my legal practice every time it comes up. We all know where you stand."

I waved my hand. "No, that's not it."

"Then what is it?" Grandma demanded.

"I wasn't including Will Hickes as one of the people affected," I said. "But I bet he wished to live forever. Vampirism is how his wish manifested." I felt like a moron for not realizing it before now. "Good night, everyone. I need to get to bed. I've got a busy day tomorrow."

"A busy day destroying people's dreams, Grinch," Grandma muttered.

I glanced back at her. "I would think you'd approve of that."

Grandma perked up. "You're right. I absolutely do." She knocked on the table. "Gin."

"Cheater," Shirley proclaimed.

I disappeared into the attic before a brawl broke out in the kitchen. Sadly, it wouldn't be the first time.

The next morning, I drove straight over to Will's house to see what I could learn about his wish. I knocked on the door a few times, but there was no answer. The car was in the driveway, which made me nervous. He'd been so out of sorts during my last visit. I hoped life as a vampire wasn't too much for him to handle. Part of me worried that he'd staked himself and I'd spot a pile of dust on the kitchen floor.

I decided to sneak around to the backyard and peer into the windows. As I rounded the corner of the house, my supernatural senses kicked in. Someone was watching me. I glanced up into the trees that bordered Will's property line. There he was, poised on the top branch of a tall oak tree.

My heart seized. "Will, don't do it!"

He looked down at me and frowned. "Eden? I didn't expect to see you here."

I was relieved I'd decided to come. "Jumping won't kill you," I called up to him.

"I know," he said. "It's pretty awesome. Watch this."

He jumped.

I opened my mouth to scream but no sound came out. Good thing, too. He landed on his feet like a nimble cat and sauntered over to me.

"I've been experimenting," he said, looking pleased with himself.

"Experimenting with suicide?"

His brow creased. "Suicide? Why would I want to kill myself now that I'm immortal?"

I shrugged helplessly. "Regret?"

Will laughed. "I've been experimenting with all the awesome things I can do now that I'm a vampire. I thought it was all fangs and eternal angst, but it's so much more than that." He seemed giddy with excitement.

"I'm glad you've embraced the new you."

"Do you know I have excellent hearing now?" he asked. "I can hear my neighbors' conversations when they're inside their houses."

"Is that a good thing?" I queried.

He grinned. "Depends on the neighbor."

"Then why didn't you hear me knock?" I asked.

"I heard the knock," he said. "I thought it was my Amazon Prime delivery." He rubbed his hands together. "Want to see what else I can do?"

"As long as it doesn't involve exposed body parts or blood, sure."

Will sped away from me. He raced across the yard so fast that his body became a blur. When he finally screeched to a halt, he wasn't even out of breath.

"That's vampire speed," I said. Although I'd never seen my stepmom run like that. She was far too elegant for fast movement.

"I've never felt so alive," Will said. He inhaled deeply. "I don't even need oxygen. It just feels nice to take deep, meaningful breaths."

"I'm relieved you're feeling positive," I said. "I had my concerns."

He reached for a low branch and began performing pull-ups in quick succession. "Is that why you're here? To check on me?"

"That…and there's something I need to ask you."

Will swung himself over and onto the branch, where he now perched. "What's that?"

"I know this will sound strange, but did you make any wishes recently?"

He vaulted to the ground and stuck the landing like a gold medal-winning gymnast. "You mean like when I blow out my birthday candles?"

"Yes, any kind of wish that you made out loud," I said. "One that you declared to the universe."

"You think the universe is granting wishes now? Because I can think of a few more."

"You don't think a wish for immortality is enough?"

His startled expression told me I was right. "How'd you know?" He pulled himself back onto the tree branch.

"It explains why you're a vampire." I moved closer to the tree and leaned against the sturdy trunk. "Humans can't have eternal life, but vampires can. Your wish was granted, just not in the way you expected."

"I guess I overreached," Will admitted. "I should've been more specific." He swung his legs back and forth. "It's not like I expected it to come true. None of my other wishes in life ever have."

"You mean your parents' divorce?"

He nodded. "I used to wish every night that they'd get back together. That we wouldn't have to move." He offered a rueful smile. "Obviously, that wish wasn't granted."

"Do you think your parents made a mistake getting divorced?" I asked. "Are they unhappy now?"

Will hung his head. "No. They're both much happier now. Not that they fought a lot when I was a kid, but I guess I sensed their…dissatisfaction. With life. With each other."

"I guess it's a good thing those wishes didn't come true then." I paused. "But something bothers me about your recent wish."

He looked at me. "You think it's selfish?"

"Not necessarily," I replied. "It's just that you don't strike me as someone so thrilled with your life that you'd want to extend it into eternity."

"Gee, thanks for that assessment," Will said, but he didn't really seem offended. "I'm not so thrilled with my life, but I'd like to know I have plenty of time left to change that. And now I do."

I studied him closely. "You're still young, Will. There's plenty of time for you to have the life you want without wishing for it to go on indefinitely."

"Not with cancer there isn't."

I started. "Cancer?" His wish suddenly made perfect sense. "How long do you have?"

"Now? Forever, I guess, unless someone decides to stake me as punishment. Before I became a vampire, though, the prognosis was grim." He stopped for a moment to regain his composure. "They told me six months."

My stomach clenched. "I'm so sorry, Will."

He dropped back to the ground. "I guess you know how this happened to me."

"I have an idea. I think we might be dealing with a wish demon."

Will laughed. "Two weeks ago, I would've said you were crazy for talking about vampires and demons like they're real. Now I'm one of them."

"If it helps, you're not the only one who's been affected," I said. "There are other victims in town."

"Victims?" he echoed. "I'm not a victim. I like that my wish came true."

"You didn't wish to become a vampire."

119

"No, but I'm getting used to the idea and I've been having fun figuring out all the awesome things I can do." He cut me a quick glance. "Which begs the question—what can you do?"

I blinked. "Me?"

"You're a...? What are you again?"

"A fury," I said. "I'd rather not talk about my particular abilities."

"Why not?" His eyes shone with curiosity. "It's all so amazing."

"Furies are different," I said. "Rare. Powerful. A little scary."

Will smiled. "You don't strike me as very scary."

I decided to give him a glimpse. I focused and huge black wings sprouted from my back. Will nearly fell backward trying to put distance between us.

"Holy smokes," he said. "You can *fly*?"

"To be honest, I haven't used them very much. They're a recent addition." I willed them to disappear.

"Why wouldn't you want to use them?" Will asked. "They're the best thing I've ever seen."

I laughed. "Don't go wishing for wings now. You have enough on your supernatural plate."

"Did a wish demon do this to you?" he asked.

"No, I acquired them after I...Forget it." I thought it best not to elaborate about how I turned into a vampire using my siphoning magic and almost sucked my partner dry. "The other victims...They're human like you."

"So what happens now?" Will asked.

"I need to find the demon and put an end to the wishes."

Will's expression darkened. "What happens when you find the demon? Do you kill it?"

"That would be a last resort," I said. "Hopefully, I'll send it back to Otherworld, where it came from. I have to find it first, though. Do you remember where you were when you made your wish?"

Will stroked his chin. "Hard to say. I've made that wish every day since I got my diagnosis. In the hospital. In my house. In my car." He chuckled bitterly. "It'd be hard to retrace my footsteps on that one."

I recalled something he said the first time we spoke. "You told me that, right before you became a vampire, you went for a walk along the river."

Will brightened. "That's the right. I always go to Davenport Park when I'm feeling down. It cheers me right up."

John had visited the park right before his wish came true, and now Will. It couldn't be a coincidence.

I rested a comforting hand on his back. "There's something else to consider, Will. If I take care of the demon, then you'll…" I drew a steadying breath. "You'll revert to your original condition."

"By original, you mean the one with cancer?"

I withdrew my hand. "Yes."

He met my gaze. "And if you don't take care of the demon?"

"Then you'll remain a vampire."

"What about the others? Are they happy with the changes in their lives?"

I felt like I was about to have a debate with Uncle Moyer. *Who cares if I claim their souls if they part with them willingly and live happy lives as part of the bargain? They're willing victims.*

"It doesn't matter either way," I said. "It's too much magic. It disrupts the natural order in this world. You didn't even know about supernaturals until this happened to you. The wish demon's actions will have long-lasting effects."

Will seemed to consider my position. "I see what you mean."

"Imagine a world where everyone's wishes came true.

What happens when wishes conflict with each other? Or someone wishes for something that has the potential to hurt others?"

"Like a megalomaniac wishes for a nuclear bomb?" Will asked.

"Wow, you took it to another level with that one, but yes."

Will blew air from his nostrils. "Okay, I get it. You have to stop the demon."

"I'm glad you can see the big picture, Will." He was a good guy.

Will laughed nervously. "Well, I'd be happier if there was flexibility in this plan."

My chest tightened. I wanted to help Will in the worst way. I really did. "I'm so sorry, Will. If there was something I could do…" I trailed off. There was nothing I could do and we both knew it.

"So this is going to sound like a bizarre request, but I've chosen cremation." His voice cracked. "Would you make sure my ashes are scattered in Davenport Park? I'll sign a letter or whatever. I just don't want my parents to have them because they'll fight over them." He swallowed hard. "I want to spend eternity where I know it's peaceful."

A lump formed in my throat. "Anything you want, Will. Your wish is my command."

CHAPTER TWELVE

THE SUN'S glare was too much for me and I slid on my sunglasses in defeat.

"It's too hard to see," I said. Any other time, I relished the sun's presence, but I was scouring the river for signs of a demon. Blinding light wasn't exactly helpful.

"I agree it's not ideal," Neville said. I'd said that he could accompany me, but only because it was nothing more than a reconnaissance mission. "The good news is that the sun won't remain in this position all day. It rises in the east and sets in the west."

I lifted my sunglasses to peer at him. "I know how the sun works, Neville."

He quickly averted his gaze. "Of course, O knowledgeable one."

"Too bad there were no wish demons associated with rivers," I said. "It might have narrowed things down."

"It doesn't mean you won't find one hiding in here," Neville said. "It just means there isn't a specific type with a strong preference for rivers."

"How deep is the river?" I asked. "Maybe the demon is

lurking at the bottom where we can't see it." Not that we could see much of anything right now.

"Fifty feet in this area, so it's quite possible."

A largemouth bass broke the surface and I jumped.

Neville chuckled. "Mind the bass. They're known for their big mouths. Highly dangerous."

I glared at him. "Keep it up and you'll see how highly dangerous *I* am." My shoulders slumped. "I'm sorry, Neville. I didn't mean to snap at you." I was home less than a month and already adopting my family's social skills.

He bowed his head. "No worries, Agent Fury."

I paced back and forth. "It has to be this stretch of river that runs through the park," I said. "This is the common area."

"There's a spell I can try, if you like," Neville said.

I cast a sidelong glance at him. "What kind of spell?"

"I can take over the bass and use it to see underwater."

"Take over? Like remote control it?"

"Basically. I can steer it from one end of the park to the other and see through its eyes. Examine the depths. If a demon is hiding at the bottom, I'll see it."

I gaped at my assistant. "That's incredible. You can really do that?"

"I've only performed the spell once so far, but it was quite effective."

"What made you try a spell like that?"

Neville hesitated. "Does it matter?"

Okay, now I had to know. "Tell me."

He dug the toe of his shoe into the dirt. "I have a cat named Fiddlesticks."

I smiled. "Of course you do."

"He's an excellent companion," Neville said. "I don't know what I would do without him."

"That's how I feel about Princess Buttercup." I missed her

sleeping next to my bed. Once I was in the barn, she'd be able to resume her place by my side. The attic steps were too awkward for a hellhound of her size.

"There's a dog in the neighborhood that was giving Fiddlesticks a hard time. A German shepherd. I know most cats wouldn't think twice about giving a dog a thrashing, but Fiddlesticks isn't like that."

I thought of my grandmother's cat. I had every confidence that Candy could take down a T-Rex should the situation present itself.

"She stopped spending time in the front garden," he continued. "When I realized it was because of the dog, I devised a plan to put the dog in its place."

I studied Neville. "You couldn't just go and talk to the owner?"

"I wanted Fiddlesticks to feel empowered and to make sure the bully knew that she wouldn't be intimidated anymore."

"So you cast a spell?"

He nodded. "It took a week to perfect the spell, but I was able to see the world through her eyes. I guided her outside and waited until the dog came, as I knew he inevitably would."

"That wouldn't fly in my neighborhood. The HOA enforces the leash policy." As I knew from personal experience. "Were you able to stand up to the dog?"

"I hissed and arched my back and made a general fuss until the message was received loud and clear. The dog hasn't stepped a single paw on my property since then."

"Good for you," I said. "Fiddlesticks must've been very grateful."

"She was," he replied. "She even let me pet her that night without biting me." He smiled at the memory. "It was a good day."

"So you think you can control the fish in the same way?"

"I do." He stepped closer to the river's edge and zeroed in on the bass, which had moved slightly downriver. He rubbed his hands together and centered himself before pointing a finger at the fish. "Stars of Ouranos, align us. Winds of Anemoi, guide us. Mother Hecate, grant me the power of union, so that two may become one."

His voice was strong and powerful, which was so unlike his usual manner of speech.

Neville grew very still and his eyes snapped shut. His body twitched and I watched as the bass disappeared beneath the surface of the water. I walked along the river, trying to track the fish but soon lost sight of it. I refused to venture too far from Neville, unwilling to leave him in his spelled state.

"Anything yet?" I asked.

"No sign of any demons," Neville replied. His breathing was ragged.

"Are you okay?"

"Nothing that a donut can't fix."

I waited patiently for him to finish exploring this section of the river. Finally, his eyes sprang open.

"Nothing noteworthy, I'm afraid." His legs buckled and I managed to catch him before he fell to the ground.

"Thanks, Neville. That was impressive."

"Would have been more impressive if I'd spotted a demon." He slid to his bottom to rest on the ground.

"If it's not in the river, then it has to be somewhere else in the area." It was too much of a coincidence for those affected to have been here when they voiced their wishes. I wondered whether Mitsy was back from New York. Maybe she could identify her precise location when she made her wish.

Neville's gaze drifted to the mound. "You have been checking on the portal regularly, haven't you?"

My brow creased. "You think the portal might have opened?"

"No, but it's possible if a demon came here, it might have been drawn to the energy inside the mound and decided to linger there."

"Good thinking," I said. "You stay here and rest." I didn't wait for him to argue. I headed straight for the portal.

I stopped outside the mound and scrutinized the area before entering. No sign of any demons. The entrance seemed undisturbed and I didn't sense any unusual activity.

I exited the mound and rejoined Neville at the river. "Feeling better?"

He was back on his feet. "Ready for that donut now."

"You go ahead. I'm going to take a walk through the rest of the park and see if I can spot anything unusual." The river appeared normal. The portal was still dormant.

I had to be missing something.

"I'm happy to join you," Neville said. "It is a lovely day for a hike."

"As long as you feel up to it."

We veered away from the river and made our way through the rest of the park. I knew this land once belonged to the Davenport family and they'd had a house here, similar to the Wentworths' house where my family now lived. The Davenports, however, had donated their land to the town and the buildings had been torn down, whereas our dairy farm had been well preserved. And now I was about to give the barn a second life as my home. There was something immensely satisfying about that.

"I don't generally come to this park," Neville said. "I'll have to change that."

"It's great to have open space like this for residents to enjoy," I said. We stood on a gently sloping hill of green grass. "I guess that's why Arthur got his statue. It's a symbol of gratitude." And the view of the bay was fantastic. I thought the view from the lighthouse was enviable, but Davenport Park was a close second.

"Have you given any thought to what you would wish for?" Neville asked.

"Not really. You?"

"Of course. I came up with a short list."

I laughed. "I expect a typed and printed form on my desk by the end of the day."

"Not until I decide the order of priority," Neville said. "That will require further consideration."

"I'd start with my big feet," I said with a laugh. Although I'd always been relatively satisfied with my looks, everyone has those few negative physical traits they wish they could get rid of.

Neville glanced down at my shoes as we walked. "I suppose they are on the large side."

"See? And that's why my wish is for smaller feet." My mother would want me to add smaller hands to that statement. She was forever making comments about my big hands. I didn't even think they were particularly big. I liked the idea of smaller feet so that I had an easier time finding shoes I liked in my size. As a size ten, I didn't exactly have the cream of the crop to choose from.

"And here I expected you to say you'd wish to return to your old life in San Francisco."

"There's a part of me that would," I said, "but I've had a lot of time to think about what happened with Fergus. The FBI was right to send me to the FBM. I was a danger to my partner and others."

"Well, if it's any consolation, you're not a danger to me. I may not be a fury, but I'm a rather talented wizard."

I offered a reassuring smile. "That you are, Neville." An idea occurred to me. "Speaking of your talents, would you mind taking a look at something for me?" I pulled out my phone and swiped the screen until I found what I was looking for.

Neville studied the picture on the screen. "What am I looking at?"

"Ingredients." It was the picture I'd taken of my mother's bedroom floor. "My mother and grandmother were using them for a secret spell."

Neville took the phone to examine the image more closely. "I can think of a few possibilities."

"I can tell they're up to something, so what's the most likely option to cause trouble?"

"I'm inclined to go with invisibility," Neville said, handing back my phone. "I've used similar ingredients for the spell on the locket you're wearing, but there's a twist here."

"What is it?"

His brow furrowed. "Based on what I've seen, I think the spell is designed to make an object invisible only to a single individual."

"You mean you could've charmed this necklace so that it only made me invisible to a chosen person?"

"Exactly."

Those two were unbelievable. "Thanks, Neville. That's incredibly helpful."

We finally reached the spot at the river where we'd started.

"Well, the hike was unproductive albeit rather nice," Neville said. "I think I'll reward my efforts with a donut now. Are you coming back to the office?"

"Not now. There's something I need to take care of." I may not have found the wish demon yet, but I'd cracked the case of the secret ingredients—and now I needed to go home and crack a few skulls.

. . .

I drove straight home and marched through the front door and into the kitchen where my grandmother was in a heated conversation with Olivia.

"If it's a problem, then you need to take care of it," Grandma was telling the five-year-old child. My mother sat at the table with them, drinking coffee.

"What's the problem?" I asked. I plucked an apple from the fruit bowl and bit into it with the same steely determination I felt toward the impending confrontation with my mother and grandmother.

"Taylor keeps stealing my crayons at school," Olivia complained. "I asked her to stop, but she won't."

"And Great-Grandma is advising you to do what, exactly?" I knew it couldn't be good.

"She wants me to put a wart on Taylor's nose," Olivia said.

"Grandma! You can't have Olivia hexing her classmates. Taking crayons is a perfectly normal thing for a child to do," I said. "It's part of development."

"Stealing is part of a child's development?" Grandma queried. "No wonder society is such a mess. In my day, you stole a crayon and you lost a hand."

"You didn't have crayons in your day," I said.

"No, but we had hands."

I inhaled deeply. "Olivia, please ignore Great-Grandma's advice. Hexing your classmates is not a good idea." I faced my mother and grandmother. "And neither is hexing your neighbor."

My mother blinked innocently. "Why would we hex Mrs. Paulson? She's nosy, but she's perfectly harmless."

"I'm not talking about Mrs. Paulson and you know it." I watched them expectantly. "I know what you're doing to Dad."

My mother and grandmother exchanged guilty looks. "I

don't know what you mean," my mother said, digging her heels in.

"Stop making his glasses invisible to him," I said. "He thinks he's going senile."

They burst into laughter.

"I told you it was a good trick," Grandma said. "I did it to my cousin Edna for an entire six months and it was glorious. She ended up getting laser eye surgery so that she didn't need to look for her glasses anymore." She paused. "So one could argue that I did her a favor."

"Well, my father isn't getting laser eye surgery. He's getting cranky."

My mother stifled another giggle. "I should have set up a hidden camera so we could watch."

"Next time," Grandma said.

"There will be no next time," I said firmly. "You can't play tricks like that."

"Why not?" my mother asked. "It's funny."

"Not to him," I said. "And it sets a bad example for others." I jerked my head toward Olivia.

"Well, she didn't know about it until you opened your big mouth," Grandma said. "So maybe you're the bad influence."

I groaned. "Olivia, please don't hex Taylor. And don't follow the advice of these two. They'll lead you down the wrong path in life."

"They told me you were a stick in the mud," Olivia said, and then frowned. "But I like mud."

"Tell your father to stop kidnapping my grandson and I'll stop hiding his glasses," my mother said.

"You know about Dad?"

"I told her," Grandma said. "I caught him sneaking out the window, but he didn't see me."

"If I broker the peace, you'd better stick to the terms," I warned.

"I'll swear on a grimoire," my mother said. "Bring me one."

"Later." I retreated to the attic and flopped on the mattress. I didn't enjoy the idea of intervening in my parents' squabbles again. It reminded me too much of my childhood. Maybe Neville was right. Maybe I should change my wish to San Francisco.

"I saw your grandmother catch your father in the act," Alice said, appearing from behind a stack of boxes.

"Next time, could you keep me in the loop?"

"Of course." She floated over to the mattress. "Still tracking the demon?"

"Not very well," I said.

"Let me know if you find it," Alice said. "I know what I'd wish for."

"To be alive again?" I asked.

"No, to cross over."

I sighed. "I'm sorry, Alice. If I knew how to help you, I would." I'd tried years ago to figure out why Alice was stuck here but didn't come up with anything. There was no record of how she died and Alice didn't seem to know.

"I know, dear. You've always been unfailingly kind to me."

"That reminds me," I said. "I met another ghost recently over at a place called Evergreen. Samuel Robinson. He seems horribly lonely and I told him about you. He didn't seem to realize he could leave the property."

"Well, I wouldn't mind escorting him around town. It would be nice to meet someone new."

"I figured."

"And how about you? Did you enjoy the company of that handsome young carpenter last night?" Alice asked.

"John's a nice guy. We've agreed to be friends."

"Successful marriages have been built on less," Alice said.

"To be honest, I'm not in the market for a boyfriend or a husband, certainly not a human one."

"What's wrong with humans? We're not so bad."

"You're not, but I might be. What if I go full fury someday? I can't risk being involved with a human. It wouldn't be safe." Not to mention exposing him to my family.

Alice floated beside me. "Eden, dear. You can't live your life afraid of what *might* happen. You have to live based on what *is*." She made a ghostly effort to pat my hand. "Trust me. You'll be willing to overcome your fears for someone you really care about."

"Maybe you're right, Alice," I said. "I guess we'll have to wait and see if that day ever comes."

"If you want it to come, it'll come. When you open yourself up to the possibility, it's more likely to happen. Not quite a wish, but it works in a similar way. No demon necessary."

I smiled at her. "No demon? I like the sound of that."

"I think I'll let you ruminate on that," Alice said. "I think I'll go over to Evergreen and open myself up to new possibilities as well."

She evaporated, leaving me alone with my thoughts.

CHAPTER THIRTEEN

HEDWIG'S THEME startled me awake the next morning. I reached for my phone on the floor beside the mattress and tapped the screen.

"Everything okay, Neville?"

"There's been an attack this morning," he said.

I bolted upright. "What kind of attack?"

"From the sound of it, a shifter gone mad, but I don't know the details. Emergency services have been called to Swiss Street."

"Thanks, Neville. I'll head over now." I clicked off the phone and threw on a pair of sweatpants and a T-shirt and slid my feet into my sneakers. I climbed down the attic steps and nearly tripped on my way to the kitchen.

"What's wrong, Eden?" Aunt Thora asked. She stood at the island, spooning oatmeal into bowls.

I stopped walking and glanced down at my feet. "My sneakers are too big."

"How is that possible?" my mother asked. "I didn't think they made sneakers in a size bigger than yours." She leaned against the counter, holding a mug of coffee.

I narrowed my eyes at her. "Of course there are sneakers in larger sizes than mine. I'm not a basketball player."

"No, of course not," my mother said. "You lack the coordination for that."

"You don't make it through Quantico with a coordination issue." Anton took a bowl of oatmeal from the island and sat at the table next to Grandma.

"Thank you, Anton." I took off my sneakers and inspected the information on the heel. Yep. Size 10. "Grandma, let me try on your shoes."

Grandma was feeding banana slices to Ryan. "Not a chance. Your feet smell."

"Since when?"

"Since you were born. I can remember spraying them with Lysol."

I stood beside her at the table, dumbfounded. "You sprayed my baby feet with Lysol? You applied a dangerous chemical to sensitive baby skin?"

"What's dangerous?" Grandma said. "Your skin is fine except for those weird red bumps you're prone to. You look like you have small insects burrowing there."

I closed my eyes and silently counted to ten. "Can I please try on your shoes?"

Grandma reluctantly slipped her foot out of her brown loafer and kicked it over to me. I slid my foot inside. A perfect fit.

"What size are you?" I asked. I only remembered that her feet were the smallest of the adult women in the family.

"A lady doesn't reveal her size."

"It's your shoe, Grandma," I said. "You're not giving anything away by telling me the size of your foot."

She hesitated before finally saying, "Seven."

My feet were now three sizes smaller than yesterday. I mean, I'd always wished for smaller feet, but….

Sweet Hecate. I *did* wish for smaller feet.

I took off her shoes. "Grandma, I need to borrow a pair of your shoes. Do you own sneakers?"

Grandma's foot shot out and she reclaimed her loafer. "I think I have a pair your mother bought me when she wanted us to do aerobics together."

"Aerobics? When was that?"

"1983," Grandma said. "They're in my closet." She pushed back her chair. "I'll get them. You feed the bottomless pit."

"Why doesn't Anton feed him?" I asked.

"Because I'm feeding myself so I can get to work," my brother replied.

"Why won't you let me in your closet?" I asked. "What's in there?"

Grandma stood. "None of your business."

"You'd better not keep black magic contraband in the house," I said.

Grandma ignored me and disappeared into her room. I fed Ryan a few more slices of banana before she returned with a pair of Adidas Concords in a faux snake pattern with a Velcro strap. I balked at the sight of them.

"Those are your sneakers?"

Anton barked a short laugh.

"What? They're vintage." Grandma shoved them at me.

"How did you wear these for aerobics?" I asked.

"I didn't," Grandma said. "Why do you think they're still in pristine condition?"

Reluctantly, I put on the shoes. At least they fit. I'd have to suck it up until I could figure out what was going on.

"Why did your feet shrink?" my mother asked.

"Because she finally washed them," Grandma said.

I glared at her. "Because I wished they were smaller."

My mother turned to look at me. "You made a wish and

wasted it on smaller feet? Why didn't you wish for a boyfriend?"

"Or a more interesting personality," Grandma added.

"I would've wished for more lemon trees," Aunt Thora said.

"I didn't know I was making a wish that would actually come true," I said. "I was hunting for the wish demon."

"I guess you found it," Grandma said.

Except I didn't. I had no idea what or how my wish had come true. Where was I when I made the wish? I needed to go back to the park, but right now I had to get over to Swiss Street.

"And where do you think you're going in my shoes?" Grandma asked.

"My assistant thinks there's been a werewolf attack. I'm driving over to the scene."

"In those sneakers?" my mother asked.

"I'm not meeting a date," I said.

"Who would be foolish enough to attack anyone?" Anton asked. "They'll have the wrath of the supernatural community upon them."

"That's what I'm going to find out."

My mother motioned to the table. "Take your brother with you."

I squinted at her. "Anton works for an ad agency. I'm a federal agent. Why would I need to take my big brother with me?"

"So you don't get hurt," my mother said.

Anton glanced at her. "But it's okay for me to get hurt? I have a family."

My jaw clenched. "What does that mean? I'm dispensable because I don't?"

"Like you said, it's your job." Anton stole a few slices of banana from Ryan's tray and dropped them into his oatmeal.

"Yes, but you're a vengeance demon," I said. "You have skills, too."

"You're the one who said you didn't need me to go," Anton countered. "I'm agreeing with you."

"But now it's just insulting." I grabbed my handbag from the counter and stormed out of the house.

I got in my car and drove to Swiss Street, careful to adhere to the speed limit. The last I needed was Deputy Guthrie to pull me over. He'd relish the chance to give me a ticket.

The flashing lights ahead told me I was in the right place. I parked behind the chief's car and walked toward the ambulance.

"Agent Fury?" Chief Fox looked at me with surprise as I approached the scene.

"Hi, Chief. I heard there was an animal attack."

"I'm not really sure what we're dealing with yet." He glanced down at my shoes. "Interesting footwear."

"They're vintage." I glanced past him to see the victim being transferred to a cot. Despite the blood and gashes, he looked vaguely familiar. "Have you identified him?"

"Maxwell Egerton," the chief said. "A thirty-seven year old male. His house is there." Chief Fox inclined his head toward the brick house behind us.

"Can he talk? Did he say what happened?" I wanted to speak to Maxwell myself, but there were too many people around. I'd have to go to the hospital.

"The only word we could get out of him was wolf," the chief said. "I know wolves have been spotted in the area on occasion, but I haven't seen reports of any attacks."

I watched as Maxwell was lifted into the back of the ambulance.

"Any witnesses?" I asked.

"Nope." The chief rubbed his stubbled jaw and my attention was drawn to the dimple in his chin.

I tried to distract myself with actual work. "Any evidence at the scene?"

He squinted. "Are you checking up on me?"

"No, I'm just being nosy."

The ambulance drove off, the wail of its siren piercing the silence of the neighborhood.

"I'm going to take another look around now," the chief said.

I didn't need to search for clues. What I needed was to talk to Maxwell before the chief had a chance to dig deeper.

"Okay, I'll let you work in peace and quiet," I said.

His brow lifted. "Really?"

"Far be it for me to interfere with your duties."

"Since when?"

"Let me know what you find out," I called over my shoulder. I rushed back to my car and raced over to the hospital. I hoped Maxwell was well enough to answer questions.

By the time I arrived, he was set up in a room and hooked up to fluids and painkillers. I made it past the nurses' station without anyone noticing me, thanks to the charmed invisibility necklace.

Maxwell's eyes were closed as I approached the bed. I opened my locket to make me visible again. I didn't want to scare the guy to death.

"Maxwell?" I said softly. "Are you awake?" His face was lined with bloody scratches and a nasty gash on his shoulder peeked out from beneath his hospital gown.

His eyes fluttered open. "Yes," he croaked. "Do I know you? You look familiar."

"I live in town. I'm sure we must have seen each other before." That would explain why he looked familiar to me, too. "Are you able to tell me what happened?"

Maxwell winced and shifted slightly in the bed. "I thought I saw a man in my yard. I went outside to see if he needed help or something, but when I got out there…" He groaned and I couldn't tell whether he was in pain now or remembering the moment. "A silver wolf. Strangest thing."

"And the wolf attacked you?"

Maxwell struggled to nod. "Rabid maybe. They're running tests."

"And the wolf just ran off afterward?"

"A car…scared it," he croaked. "My neighbor."

"He must've been the one to call 9-1-1."

A woman came rushing into the room, mascara streaking her cheeks.

"Maxwell!" she said and pushed me aside to reach him. She clutched his arm and choked back a sob. "What happened, sweetheart?"

Through a haze of pain, Maxwell managed a smile. "Suzanne."

She cupped his face with her hands. "Can I kiss you or will it hurt?"

Maxwell puckered his lips, willing to risk it, and Suzanne planted a kiss on him. I suddenly realized why Maxwell looked familiar. In fact, they both did—they were the amorous couple from the bushes near the promenade. I'd stumbled upon their secret picnic.

"Suzanne?" a gruff voice called.

Suzanne jerked away from Maxwell. "Kyle?" She clenched her fists as a man appeared in the doorway. "What are you doing here?"

Kyle looked older than Suzanne with lines around his eyes and streaks of gray in his hair. "I followed you. I tried to get your attention to see where you were going in such a hurry, but you didn't see me." Kyle narrowed his eyes at Maxwell. "Who is this?"

Suzanne inched away from the bed. "Don't you recognize Maxwell?"

Kyle stepped forward to scrutinize the patient. "What happened to you, buddy?"

"He was attacked," Suzanne said. "His neighbor called me."

"His neighbor called you? Why?" Kyle looked from Suzanne to Maxwell.

"He knows Maxwell and I work together," Suzanne explained. Her anxiety was palpable.

And it seemed apparent that Kyle knew they did more than work when they were together. He reeked of wolf. I had to diffuse the situation before it ignited right here in the hospital.

"Kyle, is it?" I gave him a friendly smile. "My name is Agent Eden Fury."

Recognition flickered in Kyle's eyes. "You're Julie's cousin."

"How about you and I take a stroll down the hall and let Suzanne discuss whatever work issue she needs to with Maxwell?"

Kyle's jaw hardened, but he took a step toward the door.

"I'll only be a minute," Suzanne promised.

I guided Kyle out of the room and down the corridor until we reached an empty room. I dragged him inside and shut the door.

"You know who I am, I take it?"

He nodded. "The new FBM agent."

"Good, now I don't have to flash my badge." My blood began to boil. "What were you thinking? Do you know how many laws you've violated today? You've jeopardized this whole community."

Kyle's tough facade crumpled. "I know, believe me. I'm so sorry. He's okay, though, right? He looked okay."

"I think he'll be fine. If not, I'm sure it's something Dr. Verity can fix." As a druid, my sister-in-law had certain healing abilities. "But we can't let this go, Kyle. It's too serious."

"You don't understand. Something weird is happening."

"I sure hope so," I said, "because there isn't a good explanation for a werewolf attack."

Kyle dragged a hand through his hair. "Okay, I admit I was out of line. I had no intention of hurting him. I only meant to scare him."

"But you got carried away?"

Kyle's nostrils flared. "I smelled her all over him. *My wife*." He turned away from me, struggling to maintain his composure. "I just lost it."

"How long have you known about the affair?"

"Only a few days," Kyle said. He drew a deep breath and faced me. "They've worked together for years. I knew Maxwell had a thing for her, but I never got any sense that Suzanne was interested." His brown eyes glistened with tears. "We've always had a happy marriage. I mean, really. Not one of those fake social media marriages."

"Did something happen recently that would change that? Arguments over money or kids?"

Kyle shook his head vehemently. "Believe me. I've run through every possible scenario in my head and I come up with nothing every time."

"Have you talked to your wife about it?" Now there was a novel idea.

"I've tried to broach the subject, but she's made it clear that Maxwell is only a work colleague."

"But you sensed a change."

"It was like she went to bed one night in love with me and woke up the next morning in love with him."

That did sound strange. "Would you mind if I spoke to her about it? See what I can find out?"

Kyle frowned. "Do you really think she'll talk to you?"

"If I can't wheedle anything out of her the old-fashioned way, I have alternatives at my disposal."

Kyle gave me a crisp nod. He understood that 'alternatives' meant something supernatural. I didn't want to resort to magic to get Suzanne to talk. I preferred the human approach whenever possible—anything to avoid accessing my powers.

"Does she know that you're a werewolf?" I asked.

"No, and I don't want her to either," Kyle said. "Suzanne is human. No Sight. It would frighten her to death to know about us. She doesn't even watch horror movies."

"You don't think it's a bit unfair to marry someone without complete honesty?"

Kyle sniffed. "I generally take a blocker so I don't shift. We opted not to have kids so that wasn't a concern. It's worked really well."

"Until now," I said.

Kyle said nothing.

"I'll talk to her," I said again.

"She's the love of my life," Kyle said. "And I know I'm hers, too."

I didn't know what to say. From what I'd seen in the bushes, Maxwell and Suzanne were infatuated with each other.

"Go home, Kyle," I said. "Consider this your one free pass."

His eyes widened. "You're not going to report me?"

"Not today, but if you so much as pee against a tree, I'll hunt you down personally."

"Understood, Agent Fury." He left the room and I waited in the corridor for Suzanne to emerge from Maxwell's room.

A nurse was bound to kick her out eventually. Sure enough, twenty minutes later, Suzanne came toward me. She seemed in better spirits than when she arrived.

"Suzanne, how is he?" I asked.

She blinked, not recognizing me for a moment. "Thank you for intervening with my husband. Kyle has a jealous streak. I never knew it until recently."

Probably because he never had a reason to be jealous until recently. I didn't have time to beat around the bush. Things were getting out of hand.

"So how long have you and Maxwell been together?"

Her gaze flickered around the corridor. "Can we maybe discuss this outside?"

"Sure, I'm on my way out anyway."

We rode in the elevator and left the hospital together. Neither of us said a word until we were safely outside and out of anyone's earshot.

"I've been careless," Suzanne admitted. "I don't really know what's come over me. If Maxwell is there, I just want to be with him. Touching him. When he's not there, I just want to go and be where he is."

"Your husband said that you and Maxwell work together."

"We have for several years," she said. "I knew he was interested in me, but I'd never felt anything for him. My husband and I have had a good marriage."

"Then what changed?"

Suzanne clasped her hands in front of her. "I don't know. I just...realized that I had feelings for Maxwell. I think they'd been bubbling beneath the surface for years."

"Bubbling?" More like exploding.

"I can't explain it, really. It's like we're magnets drawn to each other." She smiled and touched her lips. "I hope they release him today. I can't stand being away from him."

"What about Kyle? He seems to know something is going on."

"Maxwell and I had just been talking last night about when I'd ask for a divorce. We'd like to be married as soon as possible."

Wow. "You don't think things are moving too fast?"

Suzanne blew a raspberry. "You sound like my sister, Bridget."

"Bridget disapproves?"

"Thoroughly. She's been baffled by this whole affair. She thinks it's temporary insanity and begged me not to sleep with him. I told her I would never do that until I was officially separated."

"And you're planning to talk to Kyle?"

"Yes, although Bridget wants me to wait. She thinks I'll go crawling back to Kyle next week when I come to my senses."

"But you don't think so?"

Suzanne's expression grew dreamy. "If you knew Maxwell the way I do, you'd understand. It's like all my dreams have come true."

Dreams—or wishes?

Kyle was right. Something weird was happening and I had a feeling I knew exactly what it was.

CHAPTER FOURTEEN

CLARA and I sat in a booth in Gouda Nuff, the downtown diner with more dishes than they could fit on the menu. I called her from the hospital parking lot to see if she wanted to meet for breakfast. We'd spent many afternoons after school in this very booth, dreaming about our future lives or moaning about our families. One of us moaned a lot more than the other, it should be said. I won't say which one.

"Kyle should know better," Clara said, after I'd filled her in on the incident.

"I'm not making excuses for his behavior," I said, "but the wolf in him was definitely triggered. According to him, he and Suzanne have been perfectly happy. No issues."

"It sounds like Maxwell made a wish for Suzanne," Clara suggested.

"That's what I think, too," I said. "I'd like to talk to Maxwell again when he's feeling better. See if he knows exactly where he was when he made the wish."

Clara slid her fork through a sausage link. "You've narrowed it down to Davenport Park, huh? That's a lot of area for the demon to hide in."

"Except most of it is open space. Neville and I checked the river and walked all around the park, but there's no sign of a demon."

"You never told Tanner that you're a fury," Clara said.

I set down my fork. "What?"

"You gave Kyle a hard time about lying to Suzanne, but you did the same thing."

"I was in high school," I objected. "I wasn't marrying him. It was different."

"So you'll tell your next human boyfriend?" Clara asked. "You're not seventeen anymore. Marriage would be a real possibility with the next guy."

"Which is why there won't be a next guy."

Clara eyed the lone pancake still on my plate. "Are you going to finish that?"

I pushed the plate closer to her. "At least one crisis has been averted this week. I was worried that my father was sliding into senility a little early."

"But he's not?"

"Just Mom and Grandma having their idea of fun."

"Thank goodness because the idea of a senile vengeance demon is one I'd rather not contemplate." Clara laughed. "Can you imagine?" She puffed out her chest and used a deep voice. "I am here to reap vengeance. Uh, but I can't remember what you did or what I'm supposed to do to you. Would you mind filling in any gaps before I exact revenge?"

"I have enough to worry about without senile supernaturals running around town."

Clara gasped. "Can you imagine your grandma with dementia?"

"Trust me, that's the kind of thought that keeps me awake at night."

Clara's phone buzzed and she checked her screen. "Sassy is going to join us, if that's okay."

147

I groaned. "Does she have to?"

"Eden, you promised."

I did promise. Sassy had proven herself to be a good friend to Clara in the years I'd been gone. I owed it to both Sassy and Clara to make an effort to get along.

"I'll be on my best behavior," I said, "but we'll have to stop talking about supernatural stuff."

"I would think you'd welcome that," Clara said. "You're the one who wanted to get away from it by moving across the country."

Clara was right. Maybe welcoming Sassy into my inner circle would be a good thing for me. She can keep me grounded in regular human life.

"Hey, girls." Sassy bounded toward the table, her high blond ponytail swinging back and forth. She scooted in the booth next to Clara.

"Did you book the ad?" Clara asked.

Sassy beamed. "Full page, just like I said."

They high-fived each other.

"How's the ad sales business?" I asked, my lame attempt at making conversation with Sassy.

"Great," Sassy said. "I just passed this month's goal. Wait until I tell Tanner. He'll be so proud of me."

At the mention of my ex, my insides curdled. Maybe I should've wished for *him* to disappear.

"That's nice," I offered weakly.

"I'm still trying to get a real story out from under Gasper," Clara said. "He's like a dog with a bone. He refuses to let anything go."

"Talk to Cal," I said. "Tell him you want a chance to prove yourself." Cal was a decent boss and I knew he had a soft spot for Clara.

"Eden's right," Sassy said. "You're way more talented than Gasper. He's only there because of family connections."

"Wow. We actually agree on something."

"We're not so different, you know," Sassy said.

"How so?" I asked. I was dying to hear her hot take on this topic.

"Clara has talked about you a lot over the years, and it seems like you and I have a lot in common." She took a sip of Clara's iced tea. "Even our taste in men."

"Bad taste," I murmured.

Sassy didn't miss the comment. "Maybe so. To be honest, I didn't really like Tanner that much in high school. I only wanted him because you had him."

I balked. "Excuse me?"

Clara's gaze darted to her friend. "Sassy, maybe now isn't the best time for an honest conversation."

I folded my arms. "No, Clara. I think this is the ideal time for an honest conversation."

Sassy settled back in her seat. "The truth is that I was jealous of you." She paused. "Well, not all of you. I mean, I preferred my body and my face." She ran her hand down the length of her ponytail. "Okay, I preferred everything about the way I looked, but you seemed to attract good people to you. Clara was your best friend. Tanner was your boyfriend."

"Tanner *wasn't* good people," I said.

"He's not a bad person," Sassy said. "He's just flawed. Anyway, I'd never had a real friend. My mom is one of those competitive women, so she didn't have any friends either. She'd make a friend and then lose her within a month because she didn't know how to behave."

"So you had no role models," I said.

Sassy shook her head. "I was following the same pattern, but I *wanted* friends. I just didn't know how to make it happen."

"You could try not sleeping with their boyfriends for starters," I said.

Sassy heaved a sigh. "I deserve that."

I pitied the pretty blonde. Maybe Clara was right about her. Maybe she'd been misunderstood.

"I was so thrilled when I got the job at the newspaper," Sassy said. "I knew Clara worked there and I was hoping this would be my chance to make a real friend."

Clara bumped her playfully. "And I think it worked out for both of us. Turns out I needed a friend, too."

My stomach knotted at the hint of my absence. I'd never forgive myself for abandoning Clara the way I did. "You know how sorry I am about that."

"She doesn't blame you, Eden," Sassy said. "She understood that you wanted to put distance between you and your family. I don't blame you. If my family were as dysfunctional as yours, I would've done the same."

"Your mom doesn't sound like a healthy relationship," I said.

"She's much better now," Sassy said. "She's been in therapy for a couple years. I've even gone with her on occasion."

Never in my wildest dreams would I have expected to return to Chipping Cheddar to an enlightened Sassafras Persimmons.

"You should put toothpaste on that zit, by the way," Sassy said.

My fingers flew instinctively to touch my face. "Where?"

"The side of your nose. It looks like an insect has burrowed under your skin."

Lovely. "Thanks for the tip."

Sassy beamed. "That's what friends do."

With a friend like Sassy, who needed a mirror?

"Watch your elbow!" someone shouted.

I craned my neck to see that a crowd had gathered in the entryway of the diner. "Isn't it past rush hour?"

Our waitress stopped at the table to refill Clara's iced tea. "Didn't you hear? Mitsy Malone is coming. She posted it online."

I surveyed the crowd. They were all here to catch a glimpse of a teenaged girl getting diner food? People were strange.

"I guess I'll go to the restroom before it gets too busy," I said.

I threaded my way through the crowd and entered the restroom. One of the stalls was out of order so I went to the next one. Although it was locked, I didn't see any feet when I peeked below the door.

"Is someone in there?" I asked, knocking. There was no answer, but I felt a presence on the other side of the door. "Listen, if you need help, let me know. I can call someone. I'm sure I have a tampon in my bag if you need one." She wouldn't be the first woman caught by surprise.

"Will you really help me?" a small voice asked.

"Of course."

The door opened a crack and a hand grabbed me and pulled me into the stall. The tips of the young woman's hair were dyed purple and she wore oversized sunglasses with a baseball hat.

I gaped at her. "Mitsy?"

She shushed me emphatically. "I don't want anyone to know I'm here."

I laughed. "Have you seen the crowd out there? I think they know."

"I only wanted to meet a friend here for coffee, but she shared my message on social media. I've been hiding in here."

"Why? I thought you liked the attention." I couldn't imagine why, but that wasn't really the point.

"I did at first, but it's gotten out of hand." She adjusted her hat. "Plus, I have stalkers now. They wait to find out where

I'm going on social media so they can follow me and take pictures." She shivered. "It's gross. I don't want to think about what happens to those photos."

"Well, you've got this disguise going on," I said. "Maybe that will be enough?"

"It isn't," Mitsy said. "I colored my hair and started wearing a baseball hat—and I don't even like baseball. No matter what I do, I get noticed." She started to cry. "And my boyfriend broke up with me."

"Because of the attention?"

She nodded, sniffing. "David said he can't live under a microscope anymore. We were going to get married."

"Oh wow. You were? When?"

"In ten years." Her cries turned into anguished moans.

"Ten years?"

"That's been our plan. Enough time for me to get my YouTube career off the ground."

I put an arm around her. "It's going to be okay, Mitsy." As soon as I took care of this demon, it would all be okay.

"How do I stop the ride?" she choked out. "I want to get off."

I grabbed toilet paper off the roll and handed it to her to blow her nose. "I think it will all be over soon."

She peered at me from beneath the brim of her hat. "You think so?"

"Consider it your fifteen minutes of fame." No need to tell her about the supernatural world. The girl was freaked out enough. "This might seem like a weird question, but do you happen to remember where you were when you wished to be famous?"

She wiped her eyes with the toilet paper, leaving streaks of mascara on her face. "I've wanted to be famous since I was a little girl. I used to make videos of myself with my dolls."

"Any recent wishes?" I asked. "Out loud?"

Mitsy looked thoughtful. "My boyfriend and I celebrated my birthday a couple weeks ago."

"And you made a wish?"

"Sort of," she replied. "He took me to Davenport Park for a picnic. I was annoyed at first because I hate sitting on the ground." She scrunched her nose. "It's always hard and lumpy. But he was so sweet. He brought me one of those huge cupcakes from the bakery with a candle on it and sang to me."

"He sounds pretty great. I can understand why you'd want to hold on to him."

She smiled at me through her tears. "My birthday wish was to be famous. That was what I told him."

Davenport Park. No surprise there.

"Can you tell me where exactly you had your picnic?" I asked. "I'm always looking for a good spot for a picnic."

"I'm not sure," Mitsy said.

"Were you near the river?"

"No, it was further into the park. David blindfolded me until we got there because he wanted it to be a surprise. I tripped like ten times on the way there." She sighed. "But he caught me every time. That's how you know it's love—he catches you when you fall."

"That's a nice sentiment," I said. "I'll tell you what. I'm going to help you get out of here sight unseen."

"How do you expect to do that? It's mobbed out there."

"You'll have to trust me." I unclasped the locket from around my neck and handed it to her. "Wear this until you get outside. No one will recognize you."

She scrutinized the necklace. "Because I would never wear such an ugly necklace?"

"Exactly."

She hung it around her neck and I closed the locket. "I

don't know which is worse," she said, "this necklace or the baseball hat."

I opened the stall door. "Come on. I'll walk you out and make sure no one notices you. Then I'll take my necklace back." I'd have to text Clara from outside. She would understand.

"Are you sure you want it back? We can just throw it away."

"It has sentimental value," I lied.

We vacated the stall and maneuvered our way through the bodies. It seemed more crowded than when I entered the restroom.

"This is great," Mitsy whispered. "No one's noticed me."

We made it to the door and walked down the sidewalk until we could turn safely into an alley. Mitsy pulled the jewelry over her head and handed it to me.

"Thanks," she said. "That ugly necklace worked like a charm."

I smiled and placed the locket back around my neck. "It sure did."

CHAPTER FIFTEEN

I RETURNED to the hospital to check on Maxwell and discovered that he'd been discharged. I wasted no time in heading over to Swiss Street. Maxwell was my last hope to find the wish demon.

I knocked on the door and waited patiently. Maxwell had been pretty roughed up. He was unlikely to move quickly.

The door opened a crack and Maxwell peered outside. His skin was still streaked with scratches, but they appeared to be healing quickly. He frowned at the sight of me.

"You again? This is getting to be a habit."

I flashed my badge. To a human like Maxwell, it looked like an official FBI badge.

"Maxwell, my name is Agent Eden Fury. We spoke a bit in the hospital, but you obviously weren't feeling well. Would you be able to answer a few questions now?"

Maxwell hesitated. "The FBI is interested in a wolf attack?"

"I'd explain, but our reasons are classified," I said.

Maxwell pulled the door open and stepped aside. "Please come in, Agent Fury."

I crossed the threshold and surveyed the tidy interior. "How are you feeling? You look much better."

"I feel much better, thank you," Maxwell said. "Can I offer you anything? I have lots of herbal tea."

"Please don't wait on me," I said. "Let's go sit down so you can rest. I'm sure you're still tired."

Maxwell offered a weak smile and shuffled into the living room. The room was sparsely decorated with white paint on the walls and no personal effects. A brown leather sofa was positioned directly in front of the television with a recliner on an angle close to the fireplace. A single end table to the right of the sofa featured a box of tissues, a mug on a coaster, and Maxwell's phone.

"How long have you lived here?" I asked. I sat on the edge of the recliner, not wanting to tip back in an undignified manner.

"Five years," he replied. He took his spot on the sofa next to the end table and checked his phone.

Five years? I would've guessed five months. "No one can accuse you of being materialistic," I said.

He glanced around the room and chuckled. "Suzanne says it's like I moved in yesterday. I told her it's been waiting for a woman's touch." His cheeks colored. "Her touch, specifically."

Something in his expression told me he wasn't simply making romantic noises. He meant it.

"How long have you been in love with Suzanne?"

"Since the moment we met three years ago." He sighed at the memory. "It was her first day at the office and we were assigned to work on a project together. It was like fate intervened and put us together. We got along like we'd known each other forever. I knew I wanted to marry her."

"Except she's already married. To Kyle."

"I had faith she'd come around eventually," Maxwell said. "A love like ours can't be contained indefinitely."

"How did you know she'd change her mind?" I asked. "Did she ever say anything to let you know she was interested?"

"Not until recently," Maxwell said. "To be honest, I'd nearly lost hope. I'd even joined one of those online dating sites. A friend convinced me to try and focus my energy on meeting other women."

"Which friend is that?"

"His name is Dom," Maxwell said. "He works with us. Poor man has watched me pine after her all this time. He and I had gone for a walk during lunch a couple of weeks ago. He was trying to convince me to move on."

"He viewed Suzanne as a lost cause?"

"Oh, for sure." Maxwell checked his phone again and smiled. "That was a text from her. She's coming by later to check on me. She's the sweetest woman in the world." He put the phone back on the end table. "Anyway, I told Dom that I would consider it, but that I wished she would finally admit she had feelings for me."

"Obviously, she did."

He beamed at me. "Happiest moment of my life. We stayed late at the office and ordered food. It was just the two of us. She'd seemed off all day and I thought she was going to tell me something horrible, but then…"

"Then what?"

"She kissed me and told me she was in love with me." His gaze swept the room. "I've pictured our photos on these walls for three years now. The idea of putting anything else up there." He shook his head. "I want this to be our home. I want evidence of our life together everywhere I look."

Wow. I couldn't imagine being in Maxwell's shoes. He'd put his life on hold for a married woman without even knowing whether she felt the same. It was either incredibly brave or incredibly foolish.

"Did she tell you what made her decide to start a romantic relationship with you after all this time?"

"She said she couldn't deny them anymore," Maxwell explained. "She'd felt nervous that whole day because she felt like something was going to happen between us and she knew it was wrong."

"But she did it anyway," I said.

He nodded, still smiling. "I cried. I actually cried from pure joy."

"I guess Dom is eating his words now," I said.

"He was definitely surprised, but he's happy for us."

"You mentioned that you and Dom went for a walk during your lunch break. Where was that?"

"Where we always go," he said. "Davenport Park. It's right near the office."

"Is there a particular spot in the park you like to go?" I asked.

"We tend to stay close to the office. It's a better view at the top end of the park anyway."

"Not near the river?"

"Sometimes we take the footpath, but we didn't that day. We stayed at the top end." He paused, appearing thoughtful. "You haven't actually asked me any questions about the attack."

"Sorry, I was just getting to that," I said quickly. "I got too caught up in your incredible love story."

He smiled. "It is incredible, isn't it? I've been pinching myself every morning since it happened."

I'd never seen anyone as lovestruck as Maxwell. Part of me regretted having to work against his interests, but his wish wasn't fair to Suzanne or Kyle.

"You said you saw someone in your yard and went outside to check it out, but ran into the wolf instead. What did the wolf do once you were outside? Did it growl or foam at the mouth?"

"I don't think so. I just remember trying to fight it off."

"And the man you saw? Do you recall what he looked like?"

Maxwell sipped his tea. "I didn't see him clearly. It was more of a silhouette. The sun was barely up at the time."

Good. That meant he didn't recognize it was Kyle. One problem dodged.

"Thanks for your help," I said. "Do you need anything before I go?"

Maxwell glanced at his phone again and smiled. "No, thank you. I have everything I need."

I returned from Maxwell's and went up to the attic for a quick rest before I headed back to Davenport Park. At least Maxwell's information helped me narrow down the area to the top end of the park.

I kicked off the vintage Adidas. My feet and legs were sore —I suspected from walking around with the wrong size feet.

Alice's head emerged from a hatbox and I screamed.

"Can you please make a noise before you pop out like a weasel?" I asked.

"I'm so sorry, dear," Alice said. "I didn't mean to frighten you."

"That's okay. I'm just in a foul mood. I need to go walk through Davenport Park again and my feet and legs are killing me."

"Ah, the Davenports. Such a nice family." She paused. "Why do they get a park and we don't?"

"Same reason Arthur gets a statue. They donated their property to the town. The park is where the farm used to be."

Alice drifted to the window. "I remember their farm. It was similar to ours, but with a better view."

"*Much* better," I agreed.

"A shame there's no barn there for you to renovate. It would put a little more distance between you and your family and give you a lovely view of the bay."

"There's nothing left there," I said. "No barn. No house. No well."

My whole body straightened.

"What is it, Eden?"

Great Goddess on a cracker. "Did the Davenports have a well?"

"I'm sure they did," Alice said. "All the farms had one. I don't know what would've happened to it once the town took over the land, though, whether it would have been filled in…"

"It hasn't been filled in." Reluctantly, I pulled the horrible shoes back onto my feet.

"How do you know?"

"Because if my theory is correct, there's a wish demon trapped at the bottom of it." A wish demon able to hear and grant the wishes of anyone passing by.

"I wonder if that's how wishing wells started," Alice said.

"I'll let you do the research on that," I said. Right now I had my own research to do.

I hurried from the attic and went in search of Princess Buttercup. If anyone could help me sniff out the location of the well, it was my hellhound.

On the way down the front porch steps, I pitched forward and shot headfirst across the lawn.

"Agent Fury, are you okay?"

I lifted my chin to see Chief Fox's shoes. Terrific. "Hi, Chief. What brings you here?"

He extended a hand and helped me up. I dusted the dirt off my clothes.

"You said to let you know about the wolf attack," he said. "We found prints, but no sign of the wolf. He must've gone back to wherever he came from."

"Thanks, that's good to know."

He hesitated. "I also wanted to apologize."

I cocked my head. "For what?"

"For Audra," he said. "Before she left, she mentioned something about your exchange in the restroom and I got the distinct impression that she was rude to you."

I started toward my car, where Princess Buttercup was waiting for me. "Don't worry about it. It's fine."

Chief Fox turned to follow me. "So you and Jim…"

"John."

"You're dating now?"

I unlocked the car door. "He's going to renovate my barn."

The chief's brow wrinkled. "That's a euphemism I haven't heard before."

"Because it's not a euphemism. He's literally going to renovate the barn out back so I can live in it."

"Oh." He scratched the back of his head. "So that was more of a work dinner?"

"I guess you can say that."

"Where are you headed now?" the chief asked.

I opened the door. "To Davenport Park with Princess Buttercup. It's a nice day. I figured I'd take a nature walk." And hunt down a wish demon in a well.

"Care for any company?"

I stared at him for an extra beat. On the one hand, I couldn't reveal what I was looking for at the park. On the other hand, Chief Fox wanted to spend time with me in the great outdoors. Alone.

"We can take my car," he added.

"Aren't you on duty?" I asked.

"I'll patrol the park," the chief said. "Like you said, it's a beautiful day. Might as well take advantage of it."

I knew I should say no, but I felt myself relenting.

"What do you say?" he asked, gesturing to his car.

"As long as I don't have to sit in the back with Princess Buttercup." I closed my car door, unable to resist.

"You can sit in the front," he said. "Handcuffs are optional."

"Fuzzy or plain?" I asked.

"I think a more appropriate question is do I have faux snakeskin to match your shoes?"

I laughed and opened the back door for the hellhound. Then I slid into the passenger seat of his car. It smelled like fresh pine and sea salt. Like him.

"You must've had this car thoroughly cleaned after Chief O'Neill died."

"What makes you say that?" he asked, as he backed out of the driveway.

"I don't smell vapor rub."

Chief Fox chuckled. "That can be arranged, if you like."

I clicked my seatbelt into place. "No thanks. I'm good with the current olfactory situation."

We drove out of Munster Close and I waved to Aggie Grace as we passed by. She was in the front yard trimming the hedges.

"So Audra's gone, huh?" I asked.

"Yes, she went back to Chicago."

"Are you two together?" I asked. Princess Buttercup stuck her head between us, as though eager to hear his answer.

"No," the chief said. He kept his eyes fixed on the road ahead.

"I thought the two of you might be getting married."

The chief began to cough and gripped the steering wheel

to keep from jerking it. "There isn't a snowball's chance of that. Ever."

My stomach slowly unknotted. "That sounds pretty definitive."

The chief pulled into the small parking lot near the park. "We've been over for a long time. To be honest, I was surprised when she said she wanted to visit. We're friends but not super close. Not like we used to be."

We got out of the car and I took Princess Buttercup by the leash until we crossed the street to enter the park. I seemed to trip every few steps. Stupid tiny feet. What made me wish for smaller feet? They couldn't even support my body size. Princess Buttercup stayed close, waiting for her orders.

"Are you having equilibrium issues?" Chief Fox asked. "You should see a doctor. It could be an inner ear thing."

"I'll talk to my sister-in-law," I said. And she'll mock my tiny feet. I was walking on the equivalent of T-Rex arms.

"Anyway, I'm sorry if Audra was rude to you. It was uncalled for."

"Do you mind me asking what appealed to you about her in the first place?" I asked. "Aside from her perfect face and body, I mean?"

He laughed. "We met when were young and I wasn't as… emotionally developed as I am now. We grew into different people over the years, but I guess our shared history kept bringing us back together."

I stopped to look at him. "You're emotionally developed, huh?"

His mouth quirked. "You beg to differ?"

"I don't know you well enough to differ."

"Well, then I guess that's what this walk is," he said. "Getting to know each other."

We passed the mound and walked alongside the river.

The current was calm today. I surveyed the area to see if I noticed anything out of the ordinary in the park. It was a little distracting having the chief beside me. I found myself sneaking glances at him as we walked. With someone that attractive, it was hard *not* to look at him.

"You don't mind if my dog gets a little exercise, do you?"

"Dogs are allowed off leash in the park," he said. "You're not breaking any rules."

I crouched down to unhook the hellhound's leash and whispered in her ear, "Find the old well, Buttercup."

Princess Buttercup barked and ran off through the park.

"She's graceful for such a big dog," Chief Fox said.

"That's a Great Dane for you," I said. I couldn't imagine what he'd say if he could see her real form.

A few minutes later, Princess Buttercup rushed toward us, barking.

"I think she wants to play," the chief said.

"She wants us to follow her." I began to jog and prayed my feet didn't betray me once again.

The hellhound stopped in the distance and I knew she'd found the well. Now I had to examine it without letting the chief know what I was up to.

The chief laughed when he noticed where Princess Buttercup was. "Did Timmy fall down the well, girl? Is that what you wanted to tell us?"

The hellhound barked.

"I heard people have been using the old Davenport well as a wishing well," I said. "Why don't we check it out?"

"Why? You plan to make a wish?"

"Seemed to work for John," I said. "He won the lottery."

"But he's still going to renovate your barn?"

"He loves what he does," I said. "I think it's great to have that kind of passion in life."

"I totally agree," the chief said. "Passion in life is critical."

I leaned over to peer down to the bottom. If I could identify the exact species, then Neville and I could figure out the best way to transport it back to Otherworld without someone getting hurt.

"Wouldn't want to fall in there," the chief said. "You can barely see the bottom. Those Davenports dug deep."

"They had deep pockets, too," I said. "That's why Arthur gets a statue but not Alice Wentworth or any of her relatives."

"Who's Alice Wentworth?"

The ghost in my attic didn't seem like the correct response. "We live on the old Wentworth dairy farm. They were one of the founding families, too."

"Cheesemakers, huh?"

I nodded and a flash of green below alerted me to a presence at the bottom of the well.

Yes! There was our demon.

I leaned further for a better view. The body was bright green with black markings. I reached for my phone to take a picture.

Big mistake.

"Yikes!" I pitched forward and nearly fell headfirst into the well. A pair of strong hands pulled me to safety.

"I've got you," the chief said.

My heart thumped in my chest. "Sorry. I leaned too far."

"I should talk to someone about having this well taken care of," the chief said. "It's a liability for the town."

"We're having ours looked at by a contractor," I said. "I can pass along his information."

"I'd appreciate it. We're lucky no one's fallen down there and gotten stuck—or worse. I'm not even sure how I'd go about getting them out."

I glanced back at the well and the knot in my stomach returned. "Me neither, Chief."

But I was about to figure it out.

CHAPTER SIXTEEN

"READ the one about the evil genius," Olivia insisted.

I'd volunteered to read bedtime stories so that Verity and Anton could go out to dinner alone. They rarely were able to spend quality time together without the children and I seized the opportunity to spend time with the kids. I aimed to be a positive force in the children's lives and that was easier to do when I was alone with them.

"How about *Monkey Train?*" I asked. "That's a cute one."

Olivia scrunched her nose. "No. That's boring."

"Ooh-ooh," Ryan said from his place on the floor. Charlemagne slithered around him in a protective circle.

"Very good, Ryan," I said. "Monkey."

"I want *Brains Are Food: A Zombie's Story*," Olivia said.

"Who bought you that?" I asked.

"Daddy brought it back from one of his trips."

Right. One of his trips to Otherworld to exact vengeance.

My phone buzzed and I glanced at the text on the screen.

"Who's Will?" Olivia asked.

I moved the phone out of her line of sight and read the text. "Double-decker crap sandwich."

"Crap," Ryan said.

"What's wrong?" Olivia asked. Even the python lifted his head to observe me.

"I need to go," I said.

"But my story!" Olivia said.

"I'll ask Mom-mom."

"You promised." Olivia began to pout.

"I'm sorry, but this is important." I felt awful, but what was happening with Will right now was too serious to ignore. "I'll send Mom-mom in."

Ryan thumped the python on the head with a rattle and Charlemagne hissed in response.

Olivia jammed a finger in the snake's face. "No hissing," she told him firmly.

I fled the room and summoned my mother to ask her to take my place. She seemed to realize the urgency of the situation because she actually refrained from making a snarky comment.

I sprinted to the car and sped over to Will's house. I practically flew to the front door and pounded on it. When he didn't answer, I forced open the door and called his name.

"Up here." His voice was shaking.

I found him upstairs, huddled in the corner of his bedroom. His face was pressed against the tops of his knees.

"Will, tell me what happened." I crouched beside him. "Did you bite her?"

He shook his head. "No, but I wanted to." Tears streamed down his face. "Like, I *really* wanted to. I almost couldn't control it."

I placed a comforting hand on his arm. "It's okay, Will. She's safe. You didn't hurt her."

"I could've killed her."

"Who was she?"

"Her name is Darcy," he said. "I met her a few weeks ago

at The Cheese Wheel and got her number, but I'd been too nervous to call."

"What changed?"

"I thought it would be cool to take a girl out while I was still a vampire," Will said. "I feel more confident than I usually do, you know?"

It made sense. Two weeks ago, he was dying from cancer. Now he was jumping from the tops of oak trees.

"We had such a fun night," he said. "I invited her back here and she said yes."

I felt a pang of sympathy. "And things got a little heated."

"In a good way," he said. "But then it was like I sensed the blood flowing through her veins. I kept kissing her neck and it was all I could do…" He trailed off and looked away. "I'm so ashamed. I would never want to hurt someone."

"And you won't," I said.

"How do you know? Did you find the wish demon?"

"Yes," I said. "I'm going to figure out the safest way to transport you tomorrow." And clearly I needed to work faster before Will's bloodlust became a real problem.

"Is there anything you can do?" he asked. "Something to make me stop craving blood?"

"Do you still have supplies?"

"Yes, your stepmom sent more blood yesterday," Will said. "She's been great."

"Good. Then you're all set." My knees cracked as I resumed a standing position. "I'm going to trap you in your house, Will. Until I can take care of the demon and get you back to normal."

"Trap me? How?"

"It's called a ward."

He stared at me. "You can do that?"

"My assistant will handle it. Neville Wyman is a wizard

and he's excellent at creating wards. It will keep everyone safe until the situation's been resolved."

Will nodded slowly. "Okay, I think that's a good plan. I don't want to be a danger to the community."

I shot off a text to Neville and explained what needed to be done. "Have you had anything to drink since you've been home?"

He ran his hands through his hair. "No, I've been too shaken up."

"Go get yourself a bottle from downstairs and then I want you to get some sleep," I said. "Your body needs more rest than you've probably been giving it."

"If I'm stuck here, I won't have much else to do anyway."

"So what happened to Darcy? She left?"

"Yeah. I told her I had a migraine and asked her to leave," Will said. "I'm sure she thinks I'm not interested." He blew out a breath. "Which is probably for the best anyway."

"Send her a text," I said. "Tell her that you're interested, and that you'll be in touch when you're feeling better."

"I have cancer, Eden," he said. "There won't be any feeling better, not after you catch your Pokémon."

I winced. "Just send the text, Will. Don't waste time worrying. If you like her, I think she deserves to hear that from you."

He pulled himself to his feet. "Okay, you're right. I'll do it."

I clapped him on the back. "Good luck with it. I'll let you know when I've taken care of the demon."

Will looked at me with a solemn expression. "You won't have to tell me, Eden. I'll know."

I was awake bright and early the next morning, determined to identify the demon responsible. I hated the idea of Will trapped in his house, scared of his own nature. To say I empathized was an understatement.

While I stared at my computer screen, the Addams Family theme song burst from my phone. I made no move to answer the call.

"Aren't you going to get that?" Neville asked.

"Nope."

"It might be important. It's playing special music."

"That music tells me how *not* important it is."

The phone continued to play the tune and Neville continued to stare at it, his discomfort rising. "You should answer. Maybe someone needs help."

"If I answer that phone, the only one that needs help will be me."

"I'm here," Neville said. "I can support you. It's in the job description."

I smiled at him. "That's very kind, but supporting me in my personal life is definitely not part of your job."

"If you just click the screen…" Neville suggested.

I groaned and tapped the screen to put Neville out of his misery. My mother's face filled the formerly blank rectangle. "What is it, Mom?"

"Finally. You never call. It's like we don't exist to you."

"We live in the same house. I saw you last night."

My mother shook her head dismissively. "Listen, your cousin Violet might have made a mess of a lesion hex on her brother and it's his school dance tonight…" I tapped the screen and she disappeared.

"Satisfied?" I asked.

Neville hesitated. "It sounds like your cousin needs help with his…lesions."

"Not my job. My work is here." I shifted my attention back to the computer screen.

"I get annoying calls, too, sometimes," Neville said.

"Congratulations." My phone rang again and I muted it. "Neville, how do I get to the database?" I clicked a few buttons on the keyboard, but the screen remained on the background image of a waterfall.

Neville came to stand beside me. "If you expect to pass for an FBI agent specializing in cyber crime, you really should know how to work a computer."

He was right. I was lucky I could operate the sun lamp that Chief Fox had given to me. It was only one switch, but I had a habit of constantly trying to push the switch in the wrong direction and then wondering why it won't budge.

"I'll be sure to practice in my spare time," I said.

Neville took the mouse and moved it to click on a folder labeled 'garbage.'

"That's the database?" I asked, incredulous. "How do you keep it from getting trashed?"

"Because the real trash folder is there and labeled as trash," Neville said, pointing to the screen.

"Can't we call the database something else?" I asked.

"Like what, Agent Fury? We need to keep it secret in the event that someone sees our computer screens."

"How about 'Neville's porn?'" No one would want to click on that.

"I think you'll find that the cyber crime division would frown upon porn on federal computers."

"But we're not really in the cyber crime division and it wouldn't be actual porn," I said. I clicked open the database.

"Click here," Neville said. "I saved the search results for types of wish demons."

I followed the link and fifty results popped up. "I can't believe there are so many different types."

"Now you'll want to cross reference wish demon with the color green," Neville advised.

I added the new search term and scanned the summaries.

"This wish demon grants the power to have one last conversation with a departed loved one." I made a sympathetic sound. "That sounds like a pretty good one."

"It depends," Neville said.

I jerked my head to look at him. "How does it depend? Isn't there someone you'd like to have one last talk with? Tell them all the things you wish you'd said when they were alive?" I didn't have that issue, of course. I could talk to ghosts, but I recognized that this was a rare ability. Besides, most people didn't want to commune with any and all ghosts, they wanted to choose which spirits to contact.

"Be careful what you wish for," Neville said. "Even a last conversation with a loved one could be damaging depending on the circumstances."

"Well, this one is definitely a bad situation all around," I said. "It's a shame because everything seemed fine initially. John had enough money to pursue his dream. Will dodged cancer. Maxwell was united with his true love. Mitsy got the fame she wanted."

"All that glitters isn't gold," Neville said.

I arched an eyebrow. "Are you going to spout platitudes at me all day?"

"I happen to be fan of platitudes. I used to own a platitude calendar. One for each day of the year."

"On the other hand, I want my feet back, so I guess they weren't all winners."

"I thought you despised your big feet," Neville said.

"They fit my body," I said. "I don't like being clumsy. It's not good for an agent to be a klutz."

"Fair point."

I continued to review the summaries and Neville returned to his desk. So many demons. So little time. Not too many green ones, though, and none that matched exactly. Strange. I clicked on the link for 'ancillary demons.'

"What's an ancillary demon?" I asked.

"Demons that are sometimes mistaken for other demons," Neville said. "They might have physical characteristics in common, much like snakes that have similar markings. One might be deadly, while the other is quite benign."

My heart jumped as I read the description of the first ancillary demon.

"Great balls of fury, Neville!"

"What is it?" He came to peer over my shoulder at the computer screen.

"It's not a wish demon," I said. "The creature in the well is something else." I pointed to the image on the screen. "It looked like this. That exact shade of green with the black markings."

"Uh oh. A scales demon?" Neville sucked in a breath. "Ooh, I don't like that. Not at all."

"You're familiar with them?"

"I've never dealt with one personally, but I know of one that caused trouble in a town in England about ten years ago."

"How do they work? They grant wishes and then turn the tables against the person who wishes?"

"Basically. The scales tip in one direction and it all looks good, then suddenly. Wham!" He smacked his hand on the desk. "They tip the other way and all hell breaks loose."

"Hence the name." I reviewed the paragraph on the screen again. "That explains what's been happening. The scales are starting to tip out of favor. If it gets any worse, things could get very ugly very fast."

"What do we do?" he asked.

"We need to figure out how to get it safely to the extraction team and returned to Otherworld without collateral damage." I reviewed all the information on the scales demon. "No arms or legs. It moves like a constrictor and can squeeze you to death if it gets around your body."

"Then we have to make sure you can handle the creature without letting it move," Neville said. He hurried to the table at the back of the office. "I have a few ideas." He began rummaging in drawers and pulling bottles from shelves.

I followed him to the table, curious to see what he was putting together. "I guess an invisibility charm won't cut the mustard this time, huh?"

"Not quite. These items will give you choices," Neville said. "You never want to embark on a mission with only a Plan A."

"Fergus used to say that, too."

He placed three bottles on the table in front of me. "This one is a Sleeping Beauty potion."

"Self-explanatory," I said.

"The downside is it takes less than a kiss to rouse it from slumber," he said. "A loud noise, for example, might be enough to break the spell."

"So there's a risk with this one."

"There are inherent risks with every potion." He tapped the lid of the round bottle in the middle. "This one is a paralysis potion. Use this if you decide to transport the demon. It will keep the creature in stasis long enough for you to hand him over to the extraction team."

"And what about this one?" I flicked the last bottle with my fingernail.

Neville looked at me. "That's a kill potion."

I snapped to attention. "You think I should kill it?"

"I wouldn't dare advise you on the course of your mission, Agent Fury."

"Eden."

"Yes, of course. Eden." He unscrewed the lid and showed me the purplish black contents. "This is called Deadly Drip.

A few drops of this on the demon's skin and it will be dead inside of a minute." He replaced the lid and set the bottle on the table.

"I guess we've got our bases covered." My gaze lingered on the Deadly Drip. I wasn't keen on killing anything and certainly not with magic. I shuddered to think which new fury power would make an appearance if I actually used my powers to kill.

"Now allow me to prepare your pack," Neville said.

"If by pack, you mean jetpack, then I'm all for it."

He gave me a deadpan look. "Your utility pack, Agent Fury."

"Be careful with the bottles," I said. "They might fall over in the backpack and spill." The last thing we wanted was to spill deadly potions where people or animals might accidentally be exposed to them.

"I have the perfect solution," Neville said. He ducked behind the table and produced—

"Is that a fanny pack?" *In the name of Nyx, please say no.*

He held up the offending item. "The bottles are the ideal size for this. You simply pop it around your waist and unzip the pack. Presto! Your bottles are accessible."

"I thought you were going to give me a cool invention."

"The fanny pack *is* a cool invention. Highly underrated, in my expert opinion."

I snapped it around my waist, unconvinced. "I feel my self-esteem plummeting by the second."

"You wear it well," Neville said.

"I've never seen James Bond wear a fanny pack," I complained.

"And I've never seen you wear a tuxedo."

I glared at him.

Neville set to work gathering the items I needed for my mission. "I have to admit, I'm relieved we're not dealing with a wish demon," he said. "I would have felt terrible about revoking their wishes. Knowing things will be careening downhill from here makes the whole thing more palatable."

"Even Cinderella didn't get to keep her coach and her beautiful dress," I said. The stroke of midnight returned the peasant girl to her former state.

Neville zipped up the backpack. "But she did get to keep a glass slipper. I doubt the demon we're dealing with allows for any such silver linings."

"I don't even want to imagine how things might get worse." Mitsy mentioned stalkers in the diner restroom. It was only a matter of time before one decided to take his obsession too far.

"Are you certain you don't want me to come with you?" Neville asked. "The park will be deserted at that hour."

"And that's the way I want it," I said. It was best to work under the cover of darkness. Less chance of being seen by humans or worse—the chief.

"You had a partner in the FBI," Neville said.

"And I nearly killed him."

"This is different," Neville said. He handed me the filled backpack.

"You're right. Now I have an assistant instead of a partner and I'm not willing to put him in any danger."

"In that case, anything else I can do to assist you?"

"Call headquarters and arrange a rendezvous so I can transfer the demon to their care."

"Here or at the well?"

"Have them meet me at the portal. It'll be too difficult to explain where the well is." It had taken me long enough to find it and I lived here.

"Ten-four, Agent Fury."

I stifled a laugh. "Ten-four? Are you on your CB radio, good buddy?"

Neville's cheeks flamed. "I saw it on a television show and found the lingo appealing."

"Let's talk like we're in the same room—because we are."

"All right then. In that case, I wish you the best of luck, Agent Fury."

I sighed. "Do me a favor, Neville. Don't wish for anything right now."

CHAPTER SEVENTEEN

MOONLIGHT STREAMED down through the trees as I made my way through the park to the well. Neville's backpack was hooked around my shoulders and the fanny pack was secure around my waist. There was no one in sight, for which I was grateful. The last thing I wanted was for someone to see me wearing faux snake sneakers and a fanny pack.

I dropped my bag to the ground and unzipped it. I removed the rope first and tied it tightly around my waist. Next I fastened a headlamp to my head and switched it on.

"The better to see you with, my dear," I said.

I pushed a stake into the ground and tied the end of the rope to it.

"I really miss drug dealers," I muttered, as I climbed over the side of the well.

"Make a wish to see them again and I can make it so," the demon replied.

I peered into the darkness of the well, trying to aim my headlamp in his direction. "No thanks. Small feet are enough."

The demon's laugh echoed in the small space. "That was you?"

I wiggled one foot in the air above his head. "Sure was. Been paying the price ever since."

"Are you coming to rescue me?" the demon asked.

"Something like that." The demon appeared to be huddled in the bottom corner. "How did you get stuck down here anyway?"

"I came from Otherworld. I'd intended to go to the Rocky Mountains. I like wide open spaces."

"One might argue this is a taste of your own medicine. Which portal did you come through?"

"New York," he said. "My cousin Ezra had done a cross-country trip and couldn't stop raving about it. I wanted to see for myself."

"Then how did you end up here?" I inched further down the side of the well, still clutching the rope.

"I felt pulled here," he said. "It was my intention to travel west, but instead I began to move south. I sensed the presence of a vortex. I thought the ley lines might converge at the bottom of this well."

"And then you got trapped down here?"

"Clearly."

"The vortex is half a mile from here," I said. "You were close."

"I would appreciate it if you could help me out of here," the demon said. "I've been quite uncomfortable."

"Try having feet too small for your body."

"That was your wish, not mine."

"Either way, I'll be glad to see the back end of you. You've done quite enough damage during your stay."

The demon laughed. "I can't help my nature."

"Of course you can," I said. "You just chose not to." I watched as his serpentine body uncoiled and slithered across the base of the well. "What do you plan to do in the Rockies?" Aside from wreak havoc whenever the opportunity presents itself.

"Explore," the demon said. "I've always wanted to explore this world. If I like it, I'll stay."

"How did you manage to get approval to come here?" Otherworld was particular about the demons it let through. A demon like this wouldn't be high on the list. Humans without the Sight would mistake them for snakes, so the physical form wasn't necessarily an issue, but their potential for long-term damage was massive.

"What makes you believe anyone gave approval?"

Ugh. Just as I suspected. He snuck in. New York was such a large portal that it was impossible for the border guards to catch every supernatural that didn't belong.

"I'll get you out of here, but you need to go home," I said. "You can't stay in this world."

"I have no interest in going home," he replied. "I'm going cross-country, as I originally planned."

"I'm afraid that's not possible," I said. "I'm an agent with the Federal Bureau of Magic and you're under my authority now." My hand slipped and I grabbed the rope, slamming into the side of the well in the process.

Ouch. That was going to leave a bruise.

"I'm under no one's authority," the demon hissed. The change in his tone told me that the friendly conversation portion of our evening had concluded.

"You have two options," I said. "You either come peacefully so I can send you back to Otherworld or I have to kill you."

"I could just agree to come peacefully so you get me out and then double-cross you."

I fixed my light on him. His green skin shimmered in the

spotlight. "Why would you admit that? Now I have no choice but to kill you."

"Hmm. Good point. My mother always said I should have more of a filter."

"As long as we're admitting things," I said, "I don't want to kill you."

"Then don't."

"But I can't let you go either."

The demon huffed. "Then I suppose that leaves us at an impasse."

A strange noise caught my attention. I looked up and noticed that the rope had begun to fray.

Sweet Hecate.

I had to move quickly before I joined the demon in the bottom of the well. He wasn't likely to be friendly once I got down there.

"Having trouble?" the demon asked.

"No, not at all," I said. "I planned for this possibility." A lie, of course. I planned for the demon's resistance, but not for a plunge to my death.

I hurriedly unzipped the fanny pack and reached for the middle bottle. The rope began to drop further and further.

"Come to papa," the demon said. He slithered beneath me and I shuddered.

I popped the lid off the bottle and dumped the contents directly onto his body. The demon began to glow.

"What did you do?" he asked. "I can't…" His next words died on his lips as his body succumbed to Neville's potion.

"Paralysis potion, to answer your question." The rope split and I fell to the bottom, landing on my bottom with a splash. The small amount of water was enough to cushion my fall.

"Blech," I said, inhaling the stench of mildew in the well. I stood and studied the demon's body next to me. It was longer than I expected. I had to figure out the best way to carry him out of the well. Actually, I had to figure out the best way out of the well—period. The rope was out of the question. If only I could levitate like Grandma. Then I remembered—I could do better than levitate.

I could fly.

I took a deep breath and willed my wings to appear. I strongly resented having to use my fury powers to get out of this predicament. The fewer reminders of my true nature, the better. I looked from side to side and saw that the tips of my wings were squashed against the interior walls of the well. It wasn't going to be easy to get out of here. Unfortunately, I didn't have a choice. The rendezvous point for the FBM extraction team was at the portal. They had no idea how to find the well.

I squatted and used my legs to lift the demon over my shoulders and place him around my neck. My father would be proud that I bent my knees so as not to strain my back. Anything to preserve my precious posture.

I nearly lost my balance under the weight of the water-logged demon. I quickly recovered and focused on moving my wings. The paralysis potion wouldn't last too long. I had to get this demon out of here and out this world.

My wings began to flap, scraping against the sides of the well. Eventually, I gained enough traction to rise. It was slow and unsteady and I nearly dropped the demon once, but I made it out of the well.

As I rose, the demon's body twitched against my shoulder. He was starting to move.

I couldn't land and walk to the mound. There wasn't time. I was going to have to fly across the park. Not ideal. The moon was still bright and I didn't have a free hand to close the invisibility locket. If anyone happened to be looking in my direction, they'd see an enormous bird carrying a snake around its shoulders. I'd have to risk it.

I flew on an angle, unable to balance the demon around my shoulders. Up ahead, I glimpsed two silhouettes, undoubtedly the extraction team. The landing was bumpy, but I made it just as the demon regained the power of movement.

The demon hissed at me as the first member of the extraction team slipped a silver collar over his head to contain him.

"Good job, Agent Fury," the other man said.

"Thanks." I willed my wings to disappear. "Tell headquarters I'll work on the paperwork tomorrow." Paperwork was my least favorite part of the job. Maybe I'd have Neville do it.

"Have a good night, Agent Fury," the second man said.

I glanced down at my still-small feet. "Out of curiosity, how long will it take the wishes to revert?"

"As soon as he's processed and crosses back to Otherworld," the first man said. "My guess is three hours, give or take?"

"Thanks." I turned and walked to my car, careful not to lose my balance.

CHAPTER EIGHTEEN

Morning sunlight streaked through the window, prompting me to wake. I sat up on the mattress and stretched my arms.

"Good morning, Eden," Alice said. "You slept well."

I cringed. "Do me a favor. Don't say the word 'well' for a few days." I flipped back the sheet to examine my feet. "Thank the gods."

"Back to a size ten?" Alice queried.

"You know my shoe size?"

"You've mentioned it often enough over the years, dear. It's a strange obsession."

As pleased as I was to have my feet restored, it was hard to think about the fallout from the reversion of the other wishes. Mitsy would fare better out of the public eye. Fame is more than it's cracked up to be anyway and I was pretty sure she'd stay out of the spotlight from now on. John also learned a valuable lesson—he discovered that he truly loved his work. Suzanne would have to rebuild her relationship with Kyle, of course. That was going to be a tough one, but at least, as a supernatural, Kyle would know what really happened and why. Although it wouldn't erase his wife's infidelity, it might help them get back to the happy couple they once were. As for Maxwell, there was no getting away from the fact that he'd be devastated. I'd have to make sure he had access to a good therapist.

And then there was Will.

I tried to ignore the guilt I felt, knowing that his cancer would be back by now. At least he could leave his house. Neville had devised the ward so that Will could break it as a human.

I got dressed and joined Verity and the kids for breakfast.

"Who would've thought an old well could cause so much trouble?" Verity said.

"I'm definitely going to make sure we hire a contractor to take care of the one here," I said. "Demons aside, I wouldn't want Olivia or Ryan to get hurt." With the amount of time Anton and I spent outside as kids, it was a wonder we'd never discovered it.

"You're a good aunt, Eden," Verity said. "I know you have mixed feelings about it, but I, for one, am glad you're home."

"Thanks, Verity." I rinsed off my bowl and spoon and put them in the dishwasher.

"Any big plans today? I suppose you deserve a day of rest."

"Nothing special," I said. "Have a good day at work."

She smiled and handed Olivia a banana. "You, too."

I slipped out of the house before anyone else saw me. I didn't want to tell my family where I was going. They'd accuse me of being a soft touch and express their disappointment in my weakness for humans. It never ceased to amaze me that supernaturals with their attitudes would choose to live among humans in the first place. I suspected it was because they liked to feel superior. In Otherworld, we all had powers and abilities. Here we were special—and didn't we all want to be special in some way?

Princess Buttercup followed me to the door, begging to accompany me. I patted her on the head. "Not this time," I said. She whined before turning away.

I got in the car and drove to Maxwell's house first. I worried about his state of mind. If I'd been given the thing I wanted most in the world, only to have it taken away—well, I sort of knew how that felt.

I knocked on the door, itching with nerves. The door opened and Maxwell stood there, fully showered and dressed.

"Hi," he said. "I was just getting ready for work. Do you need something important?"

He looked remarkably collected for a man who had his heart broken. Was it possible that he didn't know?

"I wanted to check on you," I said truthfully. "I heard that..."

His expression softened. "You heard about Suzanne reconciling with her husband, I take it."

I nodded. "I'm so sorry, Maxwell. I know how hard this must be for you."

He stepped back. "Why don't you come in? I have a few minutes before I need to go. Traffic is never bad at this hour."

I followed him into the kitchen. "Did she call you?"

"It was the oddest thing. She called in the middle of the night." He poured himself a cup of coffee. "She would sometimes text in the middle of the night, but she never called." He offered me a cup and I politely declined.

"What did she say?"

"That she woke up crying in the night and ended up having a long talk with her husband." He stopped and I sensed that he was getting choked up. "She said that she loves Kyle and wants to make it work with him. That she was sorry for misleading me."

I glanced at the bare walls in the other room—the place

he was planning to hang the framed photographs of his happy union. "How are you up and dressed? I'd be under the covers bawling my eyes out."

He smiled sadly. "I considered it, believe me, but that's not the man Suzanne fell in love with. I'd like to continue to be that man." He took a swig of coffee. "Besides, my love for her isn't predicated on her feelings for me. It's unconditional. I stayed up the rest of the night processing the news and I realized that I could live without her. I don't want to, of course, but I can and I will. Just knowing she's alive and happy." He closed his eyes briefly before opening them again. "That's enough for me."

"And you have the memories of your time together," I said. However brief.

"That I do," he said. "And trust me when I tell you I'll be replaying them in my mind whenever the need arises. If I never love another woman, I'll be satisfied with what I've been given. Some people never even get that much, you know?"

I did.

"You're an amazing man, Maxwell. Suzanne was a lucky woman."

"She still is," Maxwell said.

I gave his arm a comforting squeeze. "I'm glad you're okay."

"Would you like a cup of tea?"

"No, thanks. There's someone else I need to see."

Will's house was quiet when I approached the door. I rang the bell and crossed my fingers that he'd answer. I didn't want to break in to check on him, but I was willing.

After a couple of long minutes, the door opened. Will stood framed in the doorway. He looked...good.

"How are you feeling?" I asked.

"Pretty decent, all things considered." He opened his mouth. "My fangs are gone, so I suppose you dealt with the demon, or whatever it was."

"I did."

"Thanks for that." He paused. "I know it must've been hard for you to do that, knowing the consequences."

I leaned against the doorjamb. "It certainly wasn't easy."

"Well, I have a doctor's appointment this morning. They want to run a few tests. Now that I'm vampire-free, I figure I should get up to speed on my cancer." His throat tightened at the mention of the c-word.

"If you ever want to talk about anything that happened…" I faltered. "There are plenty of supernaturals in town that would be happy to listen. We understand how scary it must've been for you."

"Isn't this the part where you make me forget?" Will asked. "What's it called—a glamour?"

"I don't think that's necessary, do you?" I hesitated. "Unless you'd rather forget."

"What's the difference?" Will asked. "The dead don't speak, remember?"

I felt nauseous the whole way home, thinking about Will. He'd been through so much recently and now his cancer battle was about to resume. I hope he had the strength to fight.

I parked in the driveway and entered the house. It was still early enough that I expected to hear bustling in the kitchen. Instead, there was silence.

I peeked around the corner and saw that the kitchen was empty, except for Charlemagne and Candy. The python and the cat seemed to be engaged in a game of tag. I shook my head and continued toward the family room when I heard a muffled sound come from the office.

"Sshhh," I heard my mother say.

I threw open the door, expecting to see my mom and Grandma. I did not, however, expect to see Aunt Thora with them. They stood together, blocking my view of whatever was behind them.

I gaped at her. "Et tu, Aunt Thora?"

My great-aunt gave me a sheepish look. "They talked me into it."

My mother cackled. "Peer pressure? You're blaming peer pressure at your age?"

"Let's not turn on each other," Grandma said. "If we stick together, she can't crack us."

"I'm not trying to crack you," I said. "I'm trying to prevent you from getting sent to Otherworld like the scales demon."

"You wouldn't turn in your own mother," my mom said.

"Of course she would," Grandma said.

I put my hands on my hips. "There's no dark magic while I'm under your roof."

"Why do you think we're moving you to the barn?" Grandma asked.

"Besides, it isn't dark magic," my mother insisted. "It's a surprise. For you."

An unlikely story. "What kind of surprise?"

"The kind that we can't tell you about or it will spoil the fun," my mother said.

I peered at them. "I don't believe you." I continued to stand there, contemplating what to do next. After the last twenty-four hours I'd had, I didn't have it in me to deal with family drama.

Aunt Thora held out her wrists. "Go ahead and arrest me. As long as they let me keep my lemons, I'm okay with prison life."

ANNABEL CHASE

Grandma smacked her sister's bony wrists down. "No one's going to prison. Eden would never do that to us."

"Never say never," I said. "But I'll give you a pass...this time. You need to be careful, though. The new chief is young and alert. You can't flaunt your magic."

"We're not flaunting anything," my mother said. "We're in the privacy of our own home."

The doorbell rang and everyone stopped.

"Are you expecting anyone?" I asked.

"No," my mother said. "Maybe it's a delivery."

I moved the curtain to look out the window. "It's the chief."

"Did you summon him?" Aunt Thora asked.

"He's not a demon," I replied.

"Such a waste," my mother said. "Other than that, he's perfect."

"Don't even think about it," I warned her.

"Why is he here?" Grandma asked. "Quick. Cover the contraband."

I rolled my eyes. "I'll go let him in." On my way to the door, my phone bleeped. I pulled it out to see a text from Will.

Miracle on Bleu Cheese Court. In remission.

I nearly dropped the phone. *Amazing*, I typed back. *Congrats.*

I think it was the vampire blood in my system, he wrote. *Maybe it fought off the cancer?*

Take the win, I wrote. What a relief. Will deserved a miracle after all he'd been through.

I opened the door, my mood now elevated. "Top o' the morning to you, Chief." With the sunlight behind him, he looked like an angel on the doorstep. I wasn't sure what swooning actually looked like, but I was pretty sure I was doing it right now. I tried to pull myself together.

He squinted at me. "Is Fury an Irish name?"

"Do you have to be Irish to say things like 'top o' the morning?'"

He grinned. "Pretty sure it's a requirement."

"Would you like to come in? There's coffee in the pot." There was always coffee in the pot in this house because someone was always home. "It's not Daily Grind quality, but it serves its purpose."

"Don't mind if I do."

He trailed behind me into the kitchen. "What brings you here, Chief?"

"I was wondering if you heard the news about your carpenter," Chief Fox said.

I craned my neck to look at him. "You drove over here to ask me about John?"

"What about John?" my mother interjected.

Great. It seemed like my entire family had congregated in the kitchen.

"Apparently, he didn't win the lottery after all," the chief said. "It was a computer glitch."

I feigned surprise. "What a shock that must've been for him." I poured coffee into a mug that read 'caution: witches' brew' and handed it to him.

"It seems the lottery commission's lawyers reached out to him and offered him a preemptive settlement in exchange for not filing a lawsuit," the chief said.

"So he'll still get some money?" That struck me as fair.

"He doesn't need free money," Grandma said from her place at the table. "Your parents are going to pay him to renovate the barn."

"He bought a boat, didn't he?" Aunt Thora asked. "Will he get to keep it?"

"I have a feeling he was going to downsize it anyway," I said. "Life on the boat wasn't all it was cracked up to be."

"Is that why you're here?" my mother asked. "To deliver the latest town news? We have newspapers for that."

"Just a cautionary note, too," the chief said. "A resident reported sighting a large bird in Davenport Park in the middle of the night. She was out walking her dog and spotted it when the dog started cowering and crying."

Oops.

"Who walks their dog in the middle of the night?" Grandma asked. "Seems to me that's the real question."

"I don't have concerns that a giant bird is going to take off with my dog," I said. "Princess Buttercup can handle herself."

Chief Fox chuckled. "No, that's true. I just thought I'd pass along the warning is all."

"Good to know our tax dollars are going toward an over-paid harbinger," my mother said.

"Mother," I said in a low tone.

"Why do we need a new chief anyway?" Grandma added. "I think we can all agree the last one was redundant."

"Grandma," I said sharply.

"Redundant? How do you mean?" Chief Fox asked.

"We take care of our problems in this town," Grandma replied. "It's called vigilante justice and we're damn good at it."

The chief's brow lifted. "We?"

Double-decker crap sandwich. "I think I hear a siren wailing," I said, turning the chief toward the door. "Let's go see."

"The sirens haven't been seen in the Chesapeake in fifty years," Grandma said. "They prefer the Atlantic."

The chief swiveled his head to look at her. "Excuse me?"

"Grandma hasn't taken her pills yet today." I steered him out of the kitchen and back to the front porch. "Thanks so much for stopping by." I pushed him as far as the front lawn, where he dug in his heels and turned to face me with that ridiculously sexy dimpled chin.

He broke into a broad grin. "Agent Fury, I…"

"Yes, Chief?"

Princess Buttercup burst out of the house and barked.

His smile melted away. "Never mind."

I had a sneaking suspicion my mother was responsible for releasing the hound.

"I appreciate you stopping in with updates," I said. "It's good to establish a rapport for when we work together."

"Work together," he repeated. "Yeah, I guess it is."

I took a step back toward the house. "I'll be sure to watch out for large birds. Thanks for the warning."

He gave a final wave before ducking into his car. I watched him drive away, my chest aching. I couldn't cross the line with him, no matter how much I wanted to. It wasn't safe for him to get involved with me. *I* wasn't safe.

Alice appeared beside me, gazing after him. "My word. That man has the tightest bottom I've ever seen. I could bounce a wedge of cheese off it."

"Alice!"

She smiled at me. "Perhaps one day you'll get to test it for yourself, dear."

I turned back toward the house and sighed. "You never know, Alice. Sometimes wishes do come true."

* * *

Be sure to check out book 3—*No Guts, No Fury*!

ALSO BY ANNABEL CHASE

Thank you for reading *Fury Godmother*! Sign up for my newsletter and receive a FREE Starry Hollow Witches short story— http:// eepurl.com/ctYNzf. You can also like me on Facebook so you can find out about the next book before it's even available.

Other books by Annabel Chase include:

Starry Hollow Witches

Magic & Murder, Book 1

Magic & Mystery, Book 2

Magic & Mischief, Book 3

Magic & Mayhem, Book 4

Magic & Mercy, Book 5

Magic & Madness, Book 6

Magic & Malice, Book 7

Magic & Mythos, Book 8